The Adventures of Mao on the Long March

Also by Frederic Tuten

Tintin in the New World

Tallien: A Brief Romance

Van Gogh's Bad Café

The Green Hour

Frederic Tuten

The Adventures of Mao on the Long March

A NEW DIRECTIONS CLASSIC

Manufactured in the United States of America
New Directions Books are printed on acid-free paper
Originally published in 1972 by the Citadel Press, New York
First published as a New Directions Classic in 2005
Published simultaneously in Canada by Penguin Books Canada Limited
Published by arrangement with Frederic Tuten and his agent The
Watkins/Loomis Agency, New York

Library of Congress Cataloging-in-Publication Data

Tuten, Frederic.
  The adventures of Mao on the long march / Frederic Tuten.
      p. cm. -- (A new directions classic)
   Originally published: New York : Citadel Press, 1972.
   ISBN 0-8112-1632-2 (alk. paper)
  1. Mao, Zedong, 1893-1976--Fiction. 2. China--History--Long March,
1934-1935--Fiction. 3. Heads of state--China--Fiction. I. Title. II. New
Directions classics.
  PS3570.U78A64 2005
  813'.54--dc22

                            2005022152

New Directions Books are published for James Laughlin
by New Directions Publishing Corporation
80 Eighth Avenue, New York 10011

Contents

Thirty-Five Years After

A Revised Introduction to the 1997 edition of *The Adventures of Mao on the Long March*

I did not want my first novel to trade in the confidences of unhappy childhood, or to be a tale well told, peopled with colorful characters and larded with easily-prized sentiments. I was sure I did not want to do the nineteenth century novel yet once again.

That would have been to be born old and exhausted. I would be just trotting out the plaster casts and anatomical models and replaying the *Raft of the Medusa*, only in contemporary acrylic instead of venerable oils. There were some models which pointed to my novel's direction, all the same. They seemed at the time fresh and important ways of thinking about writing fiction and they seem even more relevant today.

T.S. Eliot's *The Waste Land*—its structure and not its cultural politics—was one of these models; Eliot's idea of a work composed of fragments, mosaics of quotations arranged so that their configuration transcended the parts and gave resonance to the whole, and his hint that those fragments might make up an autobiography to shore against his ruin. I was taken by the idea of an impersonal fiction, one whose personality was the novel's and not apparently that of its author, an ironic work impervious to irony, its tone a matte gun-metal gray with just a flash of color here and there to warm the reader.

In a different vein, there was the idol of my generation, Godard. I liked the anti-cinema way he sliced quotes into his narratives, and how his characters read essays and declaimed directly into the camera. Godard's radical format seemed not an end in itself, not some attempt at a purely abstract, non-referential cinema, as in the films of Stan Brakhage in America, but an essay in quickening the spent formulas of social and political cinema, and of cinema itself.

I wrote *The Adventures of Mao* at a most political time: the radical waves of '68 were hitting all shores; young people believed the Revolution was at the gate. China was near, its revolution still fresh and seemingly uncorrupted. In 1969 I published a thirty-nine page version of *The Adventures of Mao* in the magazine *Artist Slain*, one of the many items—stamps, seals, watches, rings, lithographs, cut-out figures, etc—included in a limited edition three-tier plastic box topped by Ernest Trova's sculpture, "Falling Man." Trova had asked me to write a piece on Mao's Long March for a magazine to be included among the items in the box-sculpture.

Except perhaps for length, I had no restrictions. There was a wonderful freedom in knowing that I could write as I wished, knowing that the work would be published and not be left to molder on a closet shelf among dead shoes and old diplomas. And for further encouragement, vivid experimentation was going on everywhere about me, Rauschenberg was combining disparate materials—mattresses and rubber tires, perhaps even the kitchen sink—with his paintings; Lichtenstein and his comic-book images were realigning our view of subject matter appropriate for art, and his work drove a new bright energy into painting, at a time when its vitality seemed anemic.

There was also something innovative in the literary mood of the late sixties and early seventies, some idea of refreshing the novel. (Of course, it was constantly being refreshed from the day it was born.) I'm thinking of the era of Steve Katz's *The Exaggerations of Peter Prince*, a novel interlaced with photographs and ex'd-out pages of text and of Donald Barthelme's extrapolation from Pop art, the idea that comicbook characters could live in the pages of fiction as well as any characters one could invent or model after. There were other such off-register books in and about the period. But the innovative climate, on the whole, made up only a rare exception to the general and predictable weather.

The Adventures of Mao on the Long March was my first published novel but not my first attempt at writing one. I had been trying short fiction since fifteen and wrote a novella set in Mexico when I was nineteen. Very Malcolm Lowry stuff; a young man in Mexico City—love, drink, sorrows, the obsidian night of the soul. Somehow Jack Kerouac crept into the pages as well. Then another novel went on and off in my late twenties, a story about a young man on the Lower East Side who makes his way by collecting bottles and trash, his idea to live like an urban Thoreau, to the bone and unencumbered. I intercut the narrative with passages from *Walden* and from Emerson's essays and snatches of other early American writers. My room was filled with the American Transcendentalists, and once in a while Melville would rise from his chair and cuff their ears. I published sections of the novel years later but I never finished it.

I had come to write *The Adventures of Mao on the Long March* after hearing many voices. All the way through into my early thirties I listened to John Dos Passos and Hemingway. To mix the metaphor, I'd no sooner unstick myself from the glue of Dos Passos' trilogy *USA* with its lyrical, proletarian appeal, than I'd find myself caught in Papa's tight web—designed in planes, after Cézanne. No young writer today can imagine the power Hemingway's prose had for us then. You could take one of his sentences and twist it and shake it and slice it, and it would always return to its original shape. It was you who was misshaped at the end, turning even laundry instructions into a Hemingway line. In *The Adventures of Mao*, I tried to rid myself of these siren voices by capturing them and teasing them. All those parodies of Faulkner, Hemingway, Dos Passos, Malamud, Kerouac, done in an attempt to seize their essence through homage and to trap them in my pages, and once there, forever exorcise them and their serenades. These are the arrogant things the young dream up. Murdering Papas, ingesting them and keeping their image respectfully distant. So, with its parodies and appropriations (an inventory of them is appended), its collage format and deadpan, textbook narrative describing the history of the Long March, *The Adventures of Mao* was, I hoped, a book with no detectable voice in any one line or passage but one distinctly heard humming through in the novel's structure.

It is not for me to say how well *The Adventures of Mao* holds or does not hold its center, but I hope the novel has kept its interest in these years of changing cultural temper. I still read the book as a record of sensibility, filtered through masks and quotations, and as an autobiography of thought. The real Mao embodied the Revolu-

tion with all its contradictions, his vanity dictating
its failure, intimation of which the Mao-character
in the novel glimpses. But that is just a matter of
history.

Frederic Tuten

From "Satire Without Serifs"

by John Updike

The Adventures of Mao on the Long March, by
Frederic Tuten, wears a nice comic-book jacket
by Roy Lichtenstein and is described by Susan
Sontag on the inside flap as "soda pop, a cold
towel, or a shady spot under a tree for culture-
clogged footsoldiers on the American long
march." Broken into components, the hundred
and twenty-one pages of Mr Tuten's opus con-
sist of (1) twenty-seven pages of straight history
of the Long March (October 1934–October 1935),
done in a neutral, factual tone, as by a fellow-
travelling *Reader's Digest*; (2) thirty-six and a
half pages of quotations in quotation marks, from
unidentified sources (such as, diligent research
discovers, Hawthorne's *Marble Faun*, Walter
Pater's *Marius the Epicurean*, and Engels' *Origin of the Family, Private Property, and the State*);
(3) twelve and a half pages of parody, of Faulkner,
Hemingway, Kerouac, the Steinbeck/Farrell
school, the Malamud/Bellow school, and of mod-
ern-art criticism in numerous schools; (4)
nineteen pages of a supposed interview with
Chairman Mao in 1968, in which the Chairman
reveals himself as an avid subscriber to American highbrow periodicals and a keen devotee of
Godard films and Minimal Art; (5) twenty-six
pages of what might be considered normal nov-
elistic substance—imaginary encounters and

conversations. For an example of (5): Chairman Mao is alone in his tent, after the strain of the Tatu campaign. He hears the rumble of a tank:

A tank, covered with peonies and laurel, advances toward him. Mao thinks the tank will crush him, but it presently clanks to a halt. The turret rises, hesitantly. Greta Garbo, dressed in red sealskin boots, red railwayman's cap, and red satin coveralls, emerges. She speaks: "Mao, I have been bad in Moscow and wicked in Paris, I have been loved in every capital, but I have never met a MAN whom I could love. That man is you Mao, Mao mine."

Mao considers this dialectically. The woman is clearly mad. Yet she is beautiful and the tank seems to work. How did she get through the sentries? Didn't the noise of the clanking tank treads wake the entire camp? Where is everyone?

Mao realizes the camp is empty. He is alone with Garbo. But Mao has always been more attracted to Harlow than to Garbo. What should he do not to break her romantic little heart?

"Madame, I have work to do," says Mao gently.

"It can wait till tomorrow, my love," she answers, unzipping her coveralls.

Mao thinks: "After all, I have worked hard and do deserve a rest." But an internal voice answers him: "Rest only after socialism."

"My Mao, this is no way to treat a woman who has made a long journey to be with you."

"But what of my wife?"

"Ah, that is an old bourgeois ploy, Mao mine."

Mao succumbs, and in the tent recites to her the

entirety of the famous conclusion to Pater's *The*
Renaissance, wherein we are entreated to "burn always with this hard, gemlike flame."

The whole episode is, like others in the book, charming, and it illustrates how well Mr Tuten handles deadpan fantasy; except for a rare smirk like "her romantic little heart," a chaste solemnity rules the book. The tone is hard-edged, straight, dry, lyrical—anything but facetious. The tone, and the pamphlet-like type, smooth the different textures of this outrageous collage into an oddly reasonable unity. We never doubt that a lucid intelligence is in control; unlike many experiments of fictional assemblage, *The Adventures of Mao* never sinks into self-display, never becomes the mounted Kleenexes and tangerine peels of an author's private life. Mr Tuten, in his jacket photograph, is looking not at us but at the flame of a match that is about to light his cigarette; he is wearing long hair and a wristwatch and has no biography. The contents of his book reveal nothing of him but his attitude.

But what is that attitude? What is *The Adventures of Mao* saying? Is it satirical? In general, when confronted with, say, a giant toothpaste tube of sewn canvas or a silkscreen of soup cans, we are predisposed to assume satiric content; our liberal prejudices and romantic aesthetics (in favor of trees, naked women, sunsets, and bowls of fruit) can accept any number of wry putdowns of our comfortably deplorable mass-trash society. But works viewed this way need only a glance. The more rewarding and plausible assumption, I think, is that the artist was obscurely delighted—"turned on"—by toothpaste tubes and soup cans, and that the ancient impulse of mimesis has led him to lift these things from the flow of transient impressions and to cast them into enduring form. Mr Tuten *likes* Chairman Mao, is the first message of the novel. The schoolbook account of the Long March inspires admiration on the flat level of propaganda. Subheroically (as Homer dimples Hector's heroism with glimpses of the private man), Mr Tuten portrays Mao as sensitive to criticism of his poetry, as self-doubting and diffident and erotically wistful. In one of the funniest episodes, Mao lies awake coveting Eva Braun and Mussolini's mistress ("Claretta, what was the marvellous creature but the Mediterranean itself") but *not* Mrs Roosevelt and Señora Franco ("a rosary-kissing midget, as sexy as a decayed turnip"). Mr Tuten seems to be confessing that his Mao is a figment, a poster personality in a whimsical canon; he likes him as the author of the Gospel of John liked Jesus, but with the difference that he knows the Logos is a myth. Still, this is not satire, and in Mao's spirited championing of the bourgeois avant-garde we reach a level of serious statement:

> "Pragmatically speaking, I like the opulent severity of this art, Minimal or ABC, because it both fills the imagination with the baroque by way of dialectical reaction to the absolute starkness of the object, and denudes the false in art and in life. [Such] work is like the Long March, a victory over space and time, a triumph of the necessary over the unnecessary, and, above all, it is like Marxism, or should I say like Heraclitus."

The American interviewer finds this enthusiasm "astonishing" and the Chinese interpreter exclaims, "To be honest, Chairman Mao, hearing all this talk from you confuses and disturbs me." It is, of course, impossible for Mao to be saying these things, but not—and herein the interest, the seriousness—implausible. When, in the same interview, he asserts that

> "youth is never reactionary; youth is progressive in time and hence always in the avant-garde, hence never wrong in spirit, hence *never* to be satirized,"

the statement originates from a profound depth, where the Free World's youth-proud greening merges with the mind that unleashed the Red Guards upon the entrenched Establishment of Communist China. We are confronted, in this elevation of youngness to a moral absolute, in this denial of any possibility of venerable wisdom and selective conservation, with something truly *other* than the reasonable liberalism and sentimental romanticism that have shaped our radically imperfect world.

The ideological fabric of *The Adventures of Mao* is deliciously complicated by Mr Tuten's heavy reliance, for authority in aesthetic matters, upon fusty old wizards like Hawthorne and Pater—and Pater, it should be said, holds up nobly in this curious context. Another complication is that while the battles of the Long March are presented with the heroic generality of a newspaper recap, vivid and bloody and inglorious episodes of our own Civil War, as described in Whitman's *Specimen Days* and John William De Forest's *Miss Ravenel's Conversion*, are interspersed. The warrior Mao, whose revolution, after all, was bought with millions of lives, is thus displaced, along with the Mao who, on cultural matters, declared (at Yenan in 1942):

> There is in fact no such thing as art for art's sake, art that stands above classes, art that is detached from or independent of politics. Proletarian literature and art are part of the whole proletarian revolutionary cause; they are, as Lenin said, cogs and wheels in the whole revolutionary machine.

For this implacable and dynamic dogmatism Mr Tuten substitutes a "longing for the great simple primeval things." Mao's interviewer tells him, "All your thoughts have given me the desire to be inert." Tuten's Mao is a suave decadent, whose languor, nevertheless, has a certain appositeness to revolution. The book's last sentence (quoted from Oscar Wilde's *De Profundis*) sounds a call for purification: "I feel sure that in elemental forces there is purification, and I want to go back to them and live in their presence."

So, in part, was Dada a call for purification—a purgation of cant through nonsense. Like Pop, it embraced its age's random materials with a frantic hug that transcended criticism, cynicism, or satire. Such violent gestures seem to ask for revolution in human consciousness; what they achieve is, more modestly, a refreshing of conventional artistic forms. *The Adventures of Mao on the Long March* provides an intelligent, taut, and entertaining change from conventional novels. Its substance is satisfyingly solid and satisfyingly mysterious. Like any work of art, it could not be mindlessly replicated; a sequel might slip into being a mere anthology. Nor would it be easy to locate another symbolic person as

fabulous and germane as Mao. As is, Mr Tuten's
studied scrapbook, . . . contains the live motion
of a novel within a jagged form that does "cut
the reader into awareness."

The Adventures
of Mao
on the Long
March

"A beauty show was recently organized in Belleville, one of the suburbs of Paris, by a band of painters, poets, and sculptors. Some one hundred beauties entered the lists to compete for the prizes promised. After much ceremony and suspense the first award was bestowed on a Mlle Rochet; but her pretty face fell when she discovered it to be—a fat rabbit. The second prize was carried off—or rather down—by a Mlle Roux, to wit, a bottle of strawberry syrup. This competitor was remarkable among the rest, owing to the red Phrygian cap she had donned for the occasion. The winner of the rabbit—who could not be made to understand that it was the honor of the prize, not its value, that she should consider—showed lively symptoms of resentment, until one of the artists promised to place her profile on a medallion, as a memento of her triumph, and so there was peace and happiness."

Not long after the fall of the Ch'in dynasty in 1912 and the founding of the Chinese Republic, the Kuomingtang (KMT), a nationalist party, was formed by Dr. Sun Yat-sen, who had dreamed and fought for a united, democratic China. The KMT had allowed members of the Chinese Communist Party to join its ranks on an individual basis, not as Communist representatives. From 1922 to 1927 the KMT and the Communists were in alliance, and their relationship was cordial; indeed, Dr. Sun Yat-sen was prone to favor the Reds at home—Mao Tse-tung, for example, held high office in the KMT—and to seek the aid of the Soviet Union, one of the few Western nations he believed free of imperialistic designs on China. But after Sun Yat-sen's death in 1925, the KMT became polarized: the leftist elements in the Kuomingtang allied themselves with the Communists within the party; the rightist factions—the most powerful and headstrong represented by the military leader Chiang Kai-shek and his following of young army officers—stood in fierce opposition to the radical demands of the Communist leaders, who wanted, for example, to expropriate land from the wealthy landlords while the nationalist revolution was in progress.

"The United States was paralyzed. No one knew what was happening. There were no newspapers, no letters, no dispatches. Every community was as completely isolated as though ten thousand miles of primeval wilderness stretched between it and the rest of the world. For that matter, the world has ceased to exist. And for a week this state of affairs was maintained.

"In San Francisco we did not know what was happening even across the bay in Oakland or Berkeley. The effect on one's sensibilities was weird, depressing. It seemed as though some great cosmic thing lay dead. The pulse of the land had ceased to beat. Of a truth the nation had died. There were no wagons rumbling on the street, no factory whistles, no hum of electricity in the air, no passing of street cars, no cries of newsboys—nothing but persons who at rare intervals went by like furtive ghosts, themselves oppressed and made unreal by the silence.

"And during that week of silence the Oligarchy was taught its lesson. And well it learned the lesson. The general strike was a warning. It should never occur again. The Oligarchy would see to that."

In 1927, with the leadership and organization of the Communists and revolutionary workers, the KMT took Shanghai. No sooner had the city

been won when Chiang Kai-shek, without having
consulted other officials in the KMT, turned his troops against his Communist allies and massacred them. There were more massacres, arrests, and repressions in May of that year: in Hunan, Changsha, and Canton, workers and radical intellectuals were arrested and killed. By 1928 the split between the Communists and the Kuomingtang was irreconcilable, even if in later years there would be temporary truces and coalitions in the war against the invading Japanese armies.

Even before the final break with the KMT, Mao Tse-tung had long advocated that the Communists abandon the Kuomingtang flag in their revolutionary struggle and fight solely under the Red banner. When the split occurred and was widening, Mao's own revolutionary line had been already basically formed: He believed in the developing of the Chinese peasantry as a revolutionary force in the armed Communist revolution (an idea rejected by many of his comrades, who considered the peasantry an inert, recalcitrant element unfit for revolutionary struggle, unlike, say, the newly existent urban proletariat in whom the more "classical" Chinese Communists had invested their military aspirations).

Sea gulls wheeled and swooped down to the ferry slip. Steamships and freighters seemed chill in the raw morning dawn. He wrapped his frayed grey coat closer to his body and tossed his last cigarette into a littlepool of greasy water by his feet. He picked up his battered valise and made for the diner at the foot of the pier. It was warm and steamy inside and the coffee urn hissed.

"Coffee."

"Coffee it is," said the Greek counterman.

Joe sipped at the edges of the thick-lipped

4   mug. A longshoreman came in, a bailing hook hung around his neck. Joe put a dime down on the coffee-stained counter.

"Give me a doughnut, too."

"O.K., Buddy," said the counterman, ringing up eight cents on the register. Joe pocketed the two dull pennies change.

"Any jobs around here?" Joe asked the longshoreman.

"Nothing. Unless you're here to scab."

"Not likely," Joe said, smiling.

"You from around here?"

"No, just shipped in from Seattle."

"Heard they had some trouble out there."

"Yeah; we struck and woulda won too if they didn't get the militia in."

"Dunno. We can't hold out too much longer here even without them calling in the troopers."

"You can do a lot if you got the right organization."

"Maybe. Say, are you bolshy?"

"Just a working stiff."

Joe picked up his valise.

"See you."

"Sure thing," replied the longshoreman, as Joe walked out the door and into the brightening day. He trudged twelve blocks before coming to a soot-covered storefront window with the words "Strike Center" painted in white across the glass. Two men at a long wooden table stopped whispering when he entered.

"Looking for someone?" the one with the missing arm asked.

"Yeah, Marty."

"Whoa you?"

"Tell him Joe from Seattle."

"Christ, are *you* Joe, the guy who . . . ."

"Forget that stuff."

"O.K., sure, I'll get him. He's in the back."

Joe dropped the valise and walked to the backroom.

A tall, red-haired man wearing thick spectacles was sitting behind a desk.

"Hi, Marty."

"Jesus Christ, it's you."

"Guess so."

"Howdja get out?"

"That don't matter. We got work to do."

"Get some rest first. There's a cot here."

"Fill me in first."

"Don't you ever sleep?"

"Got enough sleep in the hole."

"Did they hurt you?"

"It was bad for a while."

"What happened anyway?"

"There was a leak in the organization. They grabbed me but the others got away—Mat and Pete are somewhere in San Fernando, the rest of the boys are scattered around."

"Things are bad here too."

"Who's the guy keeping the stiffs together?"

"An old wobbly fella, been on the docks three years and the men respect him."

"Is he with us?"

"Halfway, but he don't like taking orders from no one."

"We gotta get moving," Joe said.

"What's happening?"

"The company is willing to settle tomorrow."

Marty closed the door softly behind him as Joe slunk down on the narrow cot.

Mao supported a policy of confiscation of all privately owned land and its distribution among the landless peasantry, and he believed in the formation of strong soviet bases, Communist strongholds from which the revolution could make sorties out into the nationalist and warlord ranks, gain ground slowly, extend the perimeter of the base, and deepen and broaden the revolution. Mao's vision was of a guerrilla-revolution— a revolutionary war of attrition; for Mao the human will, the power of endurance, and the hard, resolute tenacity of the individual were the motor of the revolution. Revolution meant the enervation of the enemy, the strengthening of the Red Army, the Party, and the people.

"In a dozen states the revolt flared up. The expropriated farmers took forcible possession of the state governments. Of course this was unconstitutional, and of course the United States put its soldiers into the field. Everywhere the agents-provocateurs urged the people on. These emissaries of the Iron Heel disguised themselves as artisans, farmers, and farm laborers. In Sacramento, the capital of California, the Grangers had succeeded in maintaining order. Thousands of secret agents were rushed to the devoted city. In mobs composed wholly of themselves, they fired and looted buildings and factories. They worked the people up until they joined them in the pillage. Liquor in large quantities was distributed among the slum classes further to inflame their minds. And then, when all was ready, appeared upon the scene the soldiers of the United States, who were, in reality, the soldiers of the Iron Heel. Eleven thousand men, women, and children were shot down on the streets of Sacramento or murdered in their houses. The national government took possession of the state government, and all was over for California.

"And as with California, so elsewhere. Every Granger state was ravaged with violence and washed in blood. First, disorder was precipitated by the secret agents and the Black Hundreds, then the troops were called out. Rioting and mob-rule reigned throughout the rural districts. Day and night the smoke of burning farms, warehouses, villages, and cities filled the sky. Dynamite appeared. Railroad bridges and tunnels were blown up and trains were wrecked. The poor farmers were shot and hanged in great numbers. Reprisals were bitter, and many plutocrats and army officers were murdered. Blood and vengeance were in men's hearts. The regular troops fought the farmers as savagely as had they been Indians. And the regular troops had cause. Twenty-eight hundred of them had been annihilated in a tremendous series of dynamite explosions in Oregon, and in a similar manner, a number of train loads, at different times and places, had been destroyed. So it was that the regular troops fought for their lives as well as did the farmers."

Mao's line was opposed by the leaders of the Communist Party, especially Ch'en Tu-hsiu, whose vision was essentially that of urban revolutions fought by the industrial workers, not the peasants. Ch'en Tu-hsiu wanted revolution in the cities and directed the party to that goal: a frontal assault, a cataclysm whose end would be the irrevocable, immediate destruction of Chiang Kai-shek, the KMT, and Old China.

"The studio of a sculptor is generally but a rough and dreary-looking place, with a good deal the aspect, indeed, of a stone-mason's workshop. Bare floors of brick or plank, and plastered walls; an old chair or two, or perhaps only a block of marble (containing, however, the possibility of ideal grace within it) to sit down upon; some hastily scrawled sketches of nude figures on the whitewash of the wall. These last are probably the sculptor's earliest glimpses of ideas that may hereafter be solidified into imperishable stone, or perhaps may remain as impalpable as a dream. Next there are a few very roughly modelled little figures in clay or plaster, exhibiting the second stage of the idea as it advances towards a marble immortality; and then is seen the exquisitely designed shape of clay, more interesting than even the final marble, as being the intimate production of the sculptor himself, moulded throughout with his loving hands, and nearest to his imagination and heart. In the plaster-cast, from this clay model, the beauty of the statue strangely disappears, to shine forth again with pure white radiance, in the precious marble of Carrara. Works in all these stages of advancement, and some with the final touch upon them, might be found in Kenyon's studio.

"Here might be witnessed the process of actually chiselling the marble, with which (as it is not quite satisfactory to think) a sculptor in these days has very little to do. In Italy, there is a class of men whose merely mechanical skill is perhaps more exquisite than was possessed by the ancient artificers, who wrought out the designs of Praxiteles; or, very possibly, by Praxiteles himself. Whatever of illusive representation can be effected in marble, they are capable of achieving, if the object be before their eyes. The sculptor has but to present these men with a plaster-cast of his design, and a sufficient block of marble, and tell them that the figure is imbedded in the stone, and must be freed from its encumbering superfluities; and, in due time, without the necessity of his touching the work with his own finger, he will see before him the statue that is to make him renowned. His creative power has wrought it with a word.

"In no other art, surely, does genius find such effective instruments, and so happily relieve itself of the drudgery of actual performance; doing wonderfully nice things by the hands of other people, when it may be suspected they could not always be done by the sculptor's own. And how much of the admiration which our artists get for their buttons and buttonholes, their shoe-ties, their neck-cloths, — and these, at our present epoch of taste, make a large share of the renown, —would be abated, if we were generally aware that the sculptor can claim no credit for such pretty performances, as immortalized in marble! They are not his work, but that of some nameless machine in human shape.

"Miriam stopped an instant in an antechamber, to look at a half-finished bust, the features of which seemed to be struggling out of the stone; and, as it were, scattering and dissolving its hard substance by the glow of feeling and intelligence. As the skillful workman gave stroke after stroke of the chisel with apparent carelessness, but sure effect, it was impossible not to think that the outer marble was merely an extraneous environment; the human countenance within its embrace must have existed there since the limestone ledges of Carrara were first made. Another bust was nearly completed, though still one of Kenyon's most trustworthy assistants was at work, giving delicate touches, shaving off an impalpable something, and leaving little heaps of marble-dust to attest it.

'As these busts in the block of marble,' thought Miriam, 'so does our individual fate exist in the limestone of time. We fancy that we carve it out; but its ultimate shape is prior to all our action.'

"Kenyon was in the inner room, but, hearing a step in the antechamber, he threw a veil over what he was at work upon, and came out to receive his visitor. He was dressed in a gray blouse, with a little cap on the top of his head; a costume which became him better than the formal garments which he wore, whenever he passed out of his own domains. The sculptor had a face which, when time had done a little more for it, would offer a worthy subject for as good an artist as himself: features finely cut, as if already marble; an ideal forehead, deeply set eyes, and a mouth much hidden in a light-brown beard, but apparently sensitive and delicate.

'I will not offer you my hand,' said he; 'it is grimy with Cleopatra's clay.'

'No; I will not touch clay: it is earthy and human,' answered Miriam. 'I have come to try whether there is any calm and coolness among your marbles. My own art is too nervous, too passionate, too full of agitation, for me to work at it whole days together, without intervals of repose. So, what have you to show me?'

'Pray look at everything here,' said Kenyon. 'I love to have painters see my work. Their judgment is unprejudiced, and more valuable than that of the world generally, from the light which their own art throws on mine. More valuable, too, than that of my brother sculptors, who never judge me fairly—nor I them, perhaps.'

"To gratify him, Miriam looked round at the specimens in marble or plaster, of which there were several in the room, comprising originals or casts of most of the designs that Kenyon had thus far produced. He was still too young to have accumulated a large gallery of such things. What he had to show were chiefly the attempts and experiments, in various directions, of a beginner in art, acting as a stern tutor to himself, and profiting more by his failures than by any successes of which he was yet capable. Some of them, however, had great merit; and in the pure, fine glow of the new marble, it may be, they dazzled the judgment into awarding them higher praise than they deserved. Miriam admired the statue of a beautiful youth, a pearl-fisher, who had got entangled in the weeds at the bottom of the sea, and lay dead among the pearl-oysters, the rich shells, and the seaweeds, all of like value to him now.

'The poor young man has perished among the prizes that he sought,' remarked she. 'But what a strange efficacy there is in death! If we cannot all win pearls, it causes an empty shell to satisfy us just as well. I like this statue, though it is too cold and stern in its moral lesson; and, physically, the form has not settled itself into sufficient repose.'

"In another style, there was a grand, calm head of Milton, not copied from any one bust or picture, yet more authentic than any of them, because all known representations of the poet had been profoundly studied, and solved in the artist's mind. The bust over the tomb in Grey Friars Church, the original miniatures and pictures, wherever to be found, had mingled each its special truth in this one work; wherein, likewise, by long perusal and deep love of the 'Paradise Lost,' the 'Comus,' the 'Lycidas,' and 'L'Allegro,' the sculptor had succeeded, even better than he knew, in spiritualizing his marble with the poet's mighty genius. And this was a great thing to have achieved, such a length of time after the dry bones and dust of Milton were like those of any other dead man.

"There were also several portrait-busts, comprising those of two or three of the illustrious men of our own country, whom Kenyon, before he left America, had asked permission to model. He had done so, because he sincerely believed that, whether he wrought the busts in marble or bronze, the one would corrode and the other crumble in the long lapse of time, beneath these great men's immortality. Possibly, however, the young artist may have under-estimated the durability of his material. Other faces there were, too, of men who (if the brevity of their remembrance, after death, can be augured from their little value in life), should have been represented in snow rather than marble. Posterity will be puzzled what to do with busts like these, the concretions and petrifactions of a vain self-estimate; but will find, no doubt, that they serve to build into stone-walls, or burn into quick-lime, as well as if the marble had never been blocked into the guise of human heads.

"But it is an awful thing, indeed, this endless endurance, this almost indestructibility, of a marble bust! Whether in our own case, or that of other men, it bids us sadly measure the little, little time during which our lineaments are likely to be of interest to any human being. It is especially singular that Americans should care about perpetuating themselves in this mode. The brief duration of our families, as a hereditary household, renders it next to a certainty that the great-grandchildren will not know their father's grandfather, and that half a century hence at furthest, the hammer of the auctioneer will thump its knock-down blow against his blockhead, sold at so much for the pound of stone! And it ought to make us shiver, the idea of leav-

ing our features to be a dusty-white ghost among
strangers of another generation, who will take
our nose between their thumb and fingers (as we
have seen men do by Caesar's), and infallibly
break it off if they can do so without detection!

'Yes,' said Miriam, who had been revolving
some such thoughts as the above, 'it is a good
state of mind for mortal man, when he is content to leave no more definite memorial than the
grass, which will sprout kindly and speedily over
his grave, if we do not make the spot barren with
marble. Methinks, too, it will be a fresher and
better world when it flings off this great burden
of stony memories, which the ages have deemed
it a piety to heap upon its back.'

'What you say,' remarked Kenyon, 'goes
against my whole art. Sculpture, and the delight
which men naturally take in it, appear to me a
proof that it is good to work with all time before
our view.'

'Well, well,' answered Miriam, 'I must not
quarrel with you for flinging your heavy stones
at poor Posterity; and, to say the truth, I think
you are as likely to hit the mark as anybody.
These busts, now, much as I seem to scorn them,
make me feel as if you were a magician. You
turn feverish men into cool, quiet marble. What
a blessed change for them! Would you could do
as much for me!'

'Oh, gladly!' cried Kenyon, who had long
wished to model that beautiful and most expres-
sive face. 'When will you begin to sit?'

'Poh! that was not what I meant,' said Miriam.
'Come, show me something else.'

'Do you recognize this?' asked the sculptor.

"He took out of his desk a little old-fashioned
ivory coffer, yellow with age; it was richly carved
with antique figures and foliage; and had Kenyon

thought fit to say that Benvenuto Cellini wrought this precious box, the skill and elaborate fancy of the work would by no means have discredited his word, nor the old artist's fame. At least, it was evidently a production of Benvenuto's school and century, and might once have been the jewel-case of some grand lady at the court of the de' Medici."

However, by 1930, the failure of several Communist uprisings, notably the 1927 Autumn Harvest Uprising led by Mao (on party orders, since, as has been said, Mao was diametrically opposed to the politics of frontal attack), and the collapse of the "Canton Commune," or "Canton Uprising," redirected the party line, and Ch'u Ch'in-pai, the leader of the "Putschist" policy, was suppressed. The disaster of the Ch'u Ch'in-pai policy nearly led to the destruction of the Communist Party.

"Many young men fled into the mountains to escape serving in the militia. There they became outlaws, and it was not until more peaceful times that they received their punishment. It was drastic. The government issued a proclamation for all law-abiding citizens to come in from the mountains for a period of three months. When the proclaimed date arrived, half a million soldiers were sent into the mountainous districts everywhere. There was no investigation, no trial. Wherever a man was encountered, he was shot down on the spot. The troops operated on the basis that no man not an outlaw remained in the mountains. Some bands, in strong positions, fought gallantly, but in the end every deserter from the militia met death.

"A more immediate lesson, however, was impressed on the minds of the people by the punishment meted out to the Kansas militia. The great Kansas Mutiny occurred at the very beginning of military operations against the Grangers. Six thousand of the militia mutinied. They had been for several weeks very turbulent and sullen, and for that reason had been kept in camp. Their open mutiny, however, was without doubt precipitated by the agents-provocateurs.

"On the night of the 22 of April they arose and murdered their officers, only a small remnant of the latter escaping. This was beyond the scheme of the Iron Heel, for the agents-provocateurs had done their work too well. But everything was grist to the Iron Heel. It had prepared for the outbreak, and the killing of so many officers gave it justification for what followed. As by magic, forty thousand soldiers of the regular army surrounded the malcontents. It was a trap. The wretched militiamen found that their machine guns had been tampered with, and that the cartridges from the captured magazines did not fit their rifles. They hoisted the while flag of surrender, but it was ignored. There were no survivors. The entire six thousand were annihilated. Common shell and shrapnel were thrown in upon them from a distance, and, when, in their desperation, they charged the encircling lines, they were mowed down by the machine guns. I talked with an eye-witness, and he said that the nearest any militiaman approached the machine guns was a hundred and fifty yards. The earth was carpeted with the slain, and a final charge of cavalry, with trampling of horses' hoofs, revolvers, and sabres, crushed the wounded into the ground."

Out of the shambles, Mao and others began to

develop soviet bases, defensible territories where the Red Army could repair its losses and the party rebuild itself. Nevertheless, the basic dichotomy in policy continued to exist and manifest itself in various forms, and the "seize the cities" policy was to be put into practice until after 1930.

Mao entrenched himself and a thousand of his men in the southern Kiangsi area, and eventually the entire territory fell under the domain of the Red Army. In 1930 Mao, with party approval, designated the held territory as the Kiangsi Provincial Soviet Government. From these bases Mao launched guerrilla attacks against the KMT. But again, the direct assault policy, instigated by Li Li-san, the party leader from 1929 to 1931, proved a decisive failure. The Red Army was not strong enough for such confrontation. In the vast suppressions that followed, the KMT captured and executed Mao's younger sister and his first wife, an attractive, loving girl he had fallen in love with when he was still a student.

"*An Incident*—In one of the fights before Atlanta, a rebel soldier, of large size, evidently a young man, was mortally wounded top of the head, so that the brains partially exuded. He lived three days, lying on his back on the spot where he first dropped. He dug with his heel in the ground during that time a hole big enough to put in a couple of ordinary knapsacks. He just lay there in the open air, and with little intermission kept his heel going night and day. Some of our soldiers then moved him to a house, but he died in a few minutes.

"*Another*—After the battles at Columbia, Tennessee, where we repulsed about a score of vehement rebel charges, they left a great many wounded on the ground, mostly within our range. Whenever any of these wounded attempted to move away by any means, generally by crawling off, our men without exception brought them down by a bullet. They let none crawl away, no matter what his condition."

The key to Mao's historic Long March begins at this point. The defeat of the Red forces in their second attack on Ch'angsha broke the spine of the Li Li-san policy of assault and confrontation. From September 1 to September 13, 1930, the twenty thousand soldiers of the Communist 1st and 3rd Army Corps clashed with the might of the KMT, which vastly outnumbered and out-weaponed the Communists with heavy artillery, aeroplanes, gunboats, machine guns, grenades, and incendiary bombs. The Communists fought with rifles and small arms they had picked up from the captured and dead KMT troops. They had almost no artillery support, no air power, and no automatic weapons. Three thousand Communists died in the attack, and before all could be annihilated, Mao, who all the while had been staunchly opposed to the campaign, with-drew his troops from the battle and retreated to the safety of the base in south Kiangsi.

"The mob was no more than twenty-five feet away when the machine guns opened up; but before that flaming sheet of death nothing could live. The mob came on, but it could not advance. It piled up in a heap, a mound, a huge and grow-ing wave of dead and dying. Those behind urged on, and the column, from gutter to gutter, tele-scoped upon itself. Wounded creatures, men and women, were vomited over the top of that awful wave and fell squirming down the face of it till they threshed about under the automobiles and against the legs of the soldiers. The latter bayoneted the struggling wretches, though one I saw who gained his feet and flew at a soldier's throat with his teeth. Together they went down, soldier and slave, into the welter.

"The firing ceased. The work was done. The mob had been stopped in its wild attempt to break through. Orders were being given to clear the wheels of the war-machines. They could not advance over that wave of dead, and the idea was to run them down the cross street. The soldiers were dragging the bodies away from the wheels when it happened. We learned afterward how it happened. A block distant a hundred of our comrades had been holding a building. Across roofs and through buildings they made their way, till they found themselves looking down upon the close-packed soldiers. Then it was counter-massacre."

With the failure of this campaign went, too, the dream of a Communist victory through insurrection in the urban centers. The military collapse threatened the very existence of the Chinese Communist movement; what had begun as the politics of assault ended as the strategy of defeat. The red star of Communism seemed in its nova, and now burning out. Chiang Kai-shek's white star of nationalism appeared the only significant illumination in the otherwise murky Chinese sky.

Last week I attended a program of dances and events at the Judson Armory. There was a favorable audience response to a series of exhibitions conducted by several of the younger American artists, whose work in the plastic arts has received attention in reputable and, if I may say,

significant quarters. I had been especially interested in discussing the presentation of James
Stirling Reed, an artist from Ohio, who, over the
course of three seasons in New York City, has
demonstrated an extraordinary proficiency in
the Pop, Post-Painterly Abstraction, and Light
arenas. Mr. Reed will be remembered for his bill-
board of Elizabeth Taylor smoking a Marlboro
cigarette (1964), his 80-by-20 foot peppermint-
striped canvas (1965), and his fluorescent-light
chevron series—30 chevrons of yellow light
spaced over 1000 yards of New Jersey marshes
(1966).

After a lapse of one season, Mr. Reed has returned to us perhaps a more fully matured and
independent artist (we understand that Mr. Reed
spent the 1967-68 season in deep meditation, a
period of creative and personal maturation in-
fluenced greatly by the recent current of interest
in the ancient principles of Eastern Transcen-
dentalism*). At the Judson Armory Mr. Reed ex-
plored the premises of Optional Art (some smart
money in N.Y.C. and L.A. have already taken
orders on Optional Merchandise from L.A., the
Midwest, and N.Y.C.), the forthcoming season's
new product designed to integrate audience with
artifact.

Mr. Reed appeared on the stage with two assistants who wheeled out a highly polished stain-
less-steel disc (about six feet in circumference),
suspended by a chain from a triangle. Mr. Reed
held in his hand a padded gong beater. He explained to his audience that the disc-gong was
an inert, dormant work of art that required the
active participation of a member of the audience
in order to complete the aesthetic cycle or cir-
cuit and bring the work to life. In this instance

*See last month's column, "Money to Be Made In Meditation."

it was necessary to strike or beat the gong in order to fulfill the design, and Mr. Reed himself struck the disc several times, first in rapid succession, then in slowly paced intervals. Later, Mr. Reed brought two more "objects," one of which shall be discussed here, into aesthetic existence.

Two assistants wheeled out a grey, canvas-covered box, which Mr. Reed said was "waiting to be revealed." "Sometimes art is hidden from our eyes or is in disguise, waiting to be revealed; in this instance, the participant removes the canvas cover—and that gesture is his act of revelation." Mr. Reed did not disclose what was beneath the cover, preferring, he said, to delay that event until the opening of his show in December.

Optional Art, then, depends for its existence on its owner or viewer. In traditional art the viewer's participation was limited and, ultimately, unnecessary; it was a sectarian, aristocratic art, which may have required that the participant be especially trained or educated to make an *intellectual* and *emotional* contact with the work of art. Optional art places the viewer in autonomy—gone is the tyranny of the artist, who now only *contributes* to the creation of the work but can no longer claim god-like powers. The participant can now make *his* existential commitment to any given work: his decision and depth of commitment alone decide on whether the artifact is made art. One may see this Optional Art as the herald of a new aesthetic democracy.

Market chances are promising, depending, naturally, on the fall reviews.

At the base in Kiangsi Mao entrenched his

troops and developed the stronghold militarily and politically. Peasants and soldiers were repeatedly instructed in the theory and meaning of the Communist struggle. The peasantry, which had never been so considerately treated by any occupying force before—both warlords and landlords had squeezed them dry—responded enthusiastically to the Red troops, and many later joined their ranks. While Mao (his, incidentally, was not the only soviet base in China; *several* coexisted throughout the nation) was strengthening his position, Chiang was preparing to annihilate the Communists once and for all.

In December 1930, Chiang had mobilized 100,000 men to begin the first of his five extermination campaigns against the Red base at Kiangsi. These campaigns, covering a four-year period, have come to be known as the Five Encirclements. The First Encirclement began on December 27, 1930, and ended five days later with the defeat of Chiang's forces. The 100,000 soldiers Chiang had sent against the Red base were smashed; 10,000 were captured, as was the field commander, who was later executed. At the end of the First Encirclement the Red Army had increased its arms by 6,000 enemy rifles and many million rounds of ammunition. Three thousand enemy troops joined the Red ranks.

The Second Encirclement, in 1931, brought 200,000 KMT soldiers against the 30,000 Communists. Within one month Mao's forces captured 20,000 men and as many rifles. This ended the Second Encirclement.

"The Tenth was still marching through the woods by the flank, unable to see either fortifications or enemy, when it came under the fire of artillery, and encountered the retiring stream of wounded. At this moment and for two hours afterward the uproar of heavy guns, bursting shells, falling trees, and flying splinters was astonishing, stunning, horrible, doubled as it was by the sonorous echoes of the forest. Magnolias, oaks, and beeches eighteen inches or two feet in diameter were cut asunder with a deafening scream of shot and of splitting fibres, the tops falling after a pause of majestic deliberation, not sidewise, but stem downwards like a descending parachute and striking the earth with a dull shuddering thunder. They seemed to give up their life with a roar of animate anguish, as if they were savage beasts or as if they were inhabited by Afreets and Demons."

Chiang personally led the third campaign one month after the defeat of the second. He had 300,000 men under his command and he was determined to drive the Reds back to the Kan River in one mighty push—to steamroll the Red troops rather than to pursue a hold-consolidate-and-advance strategy, which had proven ineffectual in the First and Second Encirclements.

Mao wrote of this campaign:

"The enemy's strategy in this 'suppression' campaign was to 'drive straight in,' which was vastly different from the strategy of 'consolidating at every step' that he used in the second campaign. The aim was to press the Red Army back against the Kan River and annihilate it there.

"There was an interval of only one month between the end of the second enemy campaign and the beginning of the third. The Red Army (then about 30,000 strong) had had neither rest nor replacements after much hard fighting and had just made a detour of a thousand *li* to concentrate at Hsingkuo in the western part of the soviet area, when the enemy pressed it hard from several directions.

"In this situation the plan we first decided on was to move from Hsingkuo by way of Wanan, make a breakthrough at Fut'ien, and then sweep from west to east across the enemy's rear communication lines, thus letting the enemy's main forces make a deep but useless penetration into our base area in southern Kiangsi; this was to be the first phase of our operation. Then when the enemy turned back northward, inevitably very fatigued, we were to seize the opportunity to strike at his vulnerable units; that was to be the second phase of our operations.

"The heart of this plan was to avoid the enemy's main forces and strike at his weak spots. But when our forces were advancing on Fut'ien, we were detected by the enemy, who rushed the two divisions under Ch'en Ch'eng and Lo Cho-ying to the scene. We had to change our plan and fall back to Kaohsinghsü in the western part of Hsingkuo county, which, together with its environs, was then the only place for our troops to concentrate in. After concentrating there for a day, we decided to make a thrust eastwards towards Lient'ang in eastern Hsingkuo county, Liangts'un in southern Yungfeng county, and Huangp'i in northern Ningtu county. That same night, under cover of darkness, we passed through the forty-*li* gap between Chiang Ting-wen's division and the forces of Chiang Kuang-nai, Ts'ai T'ing-k'ai and Han Te-ch'in, and swung to Lient'ang.

"On the second day we skirmished with the forward units under Shang-kuan Yünhsiang (who was in command of Hao Meng-ling's division as well as his own). The first battle was fought on the third day with Shang-kuan Yün-hsiang's division and the second battle on the fourth day with Hao Meng-ling's division; after a three-day march we reached Huangp'i and fought our third battle against Mao Ping-wen's division. We won all three battles and captured over ten thousand rifles. At this point all the main enemy forces, which had been advancing westward and southward, turned eastward. Focusing on Huangp'i, they converged at furious speed to seek battle and closed in on us in a major compact encirclement. We slipped through in the high mountains that lay in the twenty-*li* gap between the forces of Chiang Kuang-nai, Ts'ai T'ing-k'ai and Han Te-ch'in on the one side, and Ch'en Ch'eng and Lo Cho-ying on the other, and thus, returning from the east to the west, reassembled within the borders of Hsingkuo county. By the time the enemy discovered this fact and began advancing west again, our forces had already had a fortnight's rest, whereas the enemy forces, hungry, exhausted, and demoralized, were no good for fighting and so decided to retreat.

"Taking advantage of their retreat, we attacked the forces of Chiang Kuang-nai, Ts'ai T'ing-k'ai, Chiang Ting-wen and Han Te-ch'in, wiping out one of Chiang Ting-wen's brigades and Han Te-ch'in's entire division. As for the divisions under Chiang Kuang-nai and Ts'ai T'ing-k'ai, the fight resulted in a stalemate and they got away."

In spite of Mao's extraordinary success in repulsing Chiang's troops, it is likely that, eventually, by dint of numerical and technological superiority, Chiang would have pushed through to Juichin, the capital of the soviet base, had not Japanese aggression in Manchuria caused Chiang to suddenly withdraw his forces and terminate the Third Encirclement. While Chiang was occupied with the Japanese and with problems within his own political forces, Mao made use of the interval between the Third and the Fourth Encirclement to expand the territory of the soviet base and to prepare for the next siege.

Mao's success against Chiang's superior forces was based on several factors, including luck, in the form of Japanese attack. For one, the KMT had been overconfident, expecting to destroy the weaker Red Army in a matter of weeks, but they had not counted on meeting with so determined and inspired a resistance nor were they prepared to fight in the difficult mountain terrain, where the Reds would draw them deeply. Mao's guerrilla warfare sensibility had proven itself time and again. And perhaps most basic to Mao's successes, and to all his future accomplishments on The Long March, was the fact that the Reds believed in their mission, had a zeal and determination created by a vision of their objectives.

Moreover, the civilian population within the soviet base gave their sympathy and material assistance to the Red troops thanks to Mao's practical measures in land distribution among the peasants—a policy that made them fear the success of the Chiang forces lest their newly acquired land be taken from them—and to his other social and economic reforms. Mao knew the peasantry, understood their needs and problems. Unlike his more dogmatic comrades who subscribed to the classic line of a revolution made by the urban proletariat, an idea more myth than reality in regard to the Chinese situation, Mao believed the peasantry to be a potential revolutionary force, and he treated them as such.

Because the land was his before he was the

land's and because he knew that He ordained it before the sweat had lorded it over the fields and blood and the mill ginning the cotton away till spring: He knew then in that dark dusk dawn by the Wilderness (here the men had slaved and died born from the lust and blood of the men who had cursed themselves with the blessed curse of property that was only HIS property, not the men's who have lived it or those who later wrested it from them by whiskey and bribes and lies and gilded trinkets, not theirs by deeds and rights and signatures but HIS). And he knew that the man he had injured was his brother and wife and that the man who had injured him was more than his brother and wife and that the blood would be thick and incorruptible between them long after their graves had mouldered and become imperishable and immemorial dust that all dead has and would ever have become, that their blood, the blood of the victim and executioner would mingle in the sacred stream of Time, which in itself flowed in the holy veins of the universe and its beyond, so that the two, victim and executioner, would mingle in the indissoluble stream. Then he told it, the telling in itself a long sad chronicle of dissolution and grievance and burden. The spinning tale sad and immemorial, repeated and cast once and again by the ceaseless fisherman in the enduring stream.

How the land and the houses thereon and the people thereon and the animals groaning and turning in the dark Autumnal light, the births and deaths heaving in the dark Autumnal and spinning light, how the newbirths wet and slimy heaved into the ageless Grandfather land.

The sun was coppery red on the road from Natchez. She sat on the buckboard thinking: *if only he will be there waiting, and setting up house waiting for me and the young'un, Lawd, it's a hot day here, what do they call this town?...* And the driver, jogging in the shimmer of the coppery sun thinking, *Lawd, where'd she come from all this way, her enduring so, not knowing where her man's waiting, her so big with it, it's beyond a man's knowing, and more than a womanfolk's bearing... when some folks set their minds to doing a thing there's no saying where it ends.*

Ironman Whimpie stood in the doorway with a lit cigarette in his mouth, the ash falling onto razor-creased steel-gray pants, and squinted his obsidian black eyes from the coppery sun. "Get going, get moving you squirt," he hissed between his tobacco-stained teeth.

By 1932 the position of the soviet base had been considerably strengthened. Chiang responded to this renewed threat with the Fourth Encirclement, mobilizing 500,000 men against the Communists. This campaign ended in more or less a stalemate, which was broken only when the KMT embarked on a new tactic and launched the Fifth Encirclement.

Chiang's new strategy was simple: not to try to drive the Reds to the ground—a policy that by now had shown itself futile—but to strangle them in their own territory, literally, encircle them, blockade them, starve them out.

With the aid of German advisors, the KMT virtually barricaded the Kiangsi periphery with barbed-wire fences and blockhouses bristling with machine guns and light cannons. The encirclement was surprisingly effective: the Red soldiers could neither fight their usual guerrilla war of attrition nor could they, by reason of their inferior number and meager equipment, frontally assault the enemy. The spring of 1934 saw the Kiangsi base in serious difficulty; food and clothing were scarce, and salt, an increasing rarity. In the summer Mao unsuccessfully tried to break the blockade and was squeezed even further when Chiang constructed a system of roads and highways leading up to the barricaded perimeter. Within the circle, life was moribund; without, it was nourished and flourishing.

Mao realized that to remain in Kiangsi much longer would mean the certain destruction of the Communist base, and in October 1934 he decided, with one week's notice to his officers, to break through the barricade with the entire army. It is not certain whether at that time Mao had decided where he intended to take his battered troops once he broke out. Perhaps all along he knew, with the instinct for survival of migratory animals directed by tropisms as mysterious as the whole of nature, that his destiny waited 8,000 miles away, at the soviet base of Wu Ch'ichen.

Five Propositions Toward an Objectless Art '
1) In space there is only time abstracted: the dimension of space curving into time exists as its own qualitative ratio.
2) Silence is golden.
3) If art is to be more than illustration of ideas, visual expression—on the most primitive level —of stories and descriptions of events and persons, and is ever to release its own special aesthetic quality, it must yearn for the transcendental as implied in the elemental.
4) All art is bogus fabrication.
5) Cognizance precedes analysis. Reason is the articulation of our Understanding.

The Long March is already a myth; its history reads like a hard-core propaganda tract or a dream-fantasy of bedridden invalids, political prisoners, men in death cells, or of children who float on the vision of themselves as leaders of outlaw bands fighting injustice in mountain hideouts, jungle retreats, or in the routes of city sewers and aerial tracks of tenement rooftops.

Imagine all these events concentrated into one year, in one army, under one leader: Washington and his tattered men crossing the Delaware and the agonizing encampment of the foot-bleeding, frostbitten troops at Valley Forge; Columbus's voyage to America; Napoleon's wracked winter retreat from Russia; the flight of the Armenians from the Turks; the Seminole Indian Florida swamp resistance; the Lewis and Clark expedition; Hannibal's passage over the Alps; the Watts uprising; the Oklahoma migration of the 1930's; the partisan activities throughout Europe in World War II; Che's flight in Bolivia; the Confederate General Mosby's guerrilla war in Virginia, 1863; Moses and his followers fleeing the Egyptians; Castro's eighty-man invasion of Cuba, his stay in the Sierra Maestra and the subsequent military struggles; the parade of the Barnum and Bailey circus through the main street of Chicago, 1903.

"It might be supposed that the only proper judge of statues would be a sculptor, but it may be believed that others than the artist can appreciate and see the beauty of the marble art of Rome. If what is best in nature and knowledge cannot be claimed for the privileged profession of any order of men, it would be a wonder if, in that region called Art, there were, as to what is best there, any essential exclusiveness. True, the dilettante may enjoy his technical terms; but ignorance of these prevents not due feelings for Art in any mind naturally alive to beauty or grandeur. Just as the productions of nature may be both appreciated by those who know nothing of Botany, or who have no inclination for it, so the creations of Art may be, by those ignorant of its critical science, or indifferent to it.

"Art strikes a chord in the lowest as well as in the highest; the rude and uncultivated feel its influence as well as the polite and polished. It is a spirit that pervades all classes. Nay, as it is doubtful whether to the scientific Linnaeus flowers yielded so much satisfaction as to the unscientific Burns, or struck so deep a chord in his bosom; so may it be a question whether the terms of Art may not inspire in artistic but still susceptible minds, thoughts, or emotions, not lower than those raised in the most accomplished of critics.

"Yet, we find that many thus naturally susceptible to such impressions refrain from their utterance, out of fear lest in their ignorance of technicalities their unaffected terms might betray them, and that after all, feel as they may, they know little or nothing, and hence keep silence, not wishing to become presumptuous. There are many examples on record to show this, and not only this, but that the uneducated are very often more susceptible to this influence than the learned. May it not possibly be that, as Burns perhaps understood flowers as well as Linnaeus, and the Scotch peasant's poetical description of the daisy, 'wee, modest, crimson-tipped flower,' is rightly set above the technical definition of the Swedish professor, so in Art, just as in nature, it may not be the accredited wise man alone who, in all respects, is qualified to comprehend or describe.

"With this explanation, I, who am neither critic nor connoisseur, thought fit to introduce some familiar remarks upon the sculptures in Rome, a subject which otherwise might be thought to lie peculiarly within the province of persons of a kind of cultivation to which I make no pretensions. I shall speak of the impressions produced upon my mind as one who looks upon a work of art as he would upon a violet or a cloud, and admires or condemns as he finds an answering sentiment awakened in his soul. My object is to paint the appearance of Roman statuary objectively and afterward to speculate upon the emotions and pleasure that appearance is apt to excite in the human breast."

On the night of October 16, 1934, 100,000 men took the first step of The Long March. The Communists had no transportation other than their feet and a few bony horses and pack mules. Carrying not only a meager assortment of weapons but a range of domestic implements on their shoulders—sewing machines, printing presses, sections of factory equipment, pots, pans—the army and party members began to walk toward the KMT defense works, studded with concrete-bunkered machine-gun nests. The Communists did not get through the fortifications until November 29, after severe losses. One-third of the force was destroyed and tons of equipment had to be abandoned or hidden in caches.

One afternoon as Mao trudged along at the

head of his troops in a dreamy way, he was hailed by an old friend of his student days in Peiping.

"Ola," Mao called out, remembering his friend and the hours spent with him arguing over such matters as: how best should China rid herself of foreigners; does all action undergo—by the very nature of action itself — moral disintegration; can one live in a bad society and still be a good man; for what does one live?

Yet, for all their talk, these young men had not known, in all those smoky, tea-soaked nights, that "the tranquility of the best-ordered society may be disturbed, at any time, by a sudden outbreak of the malcontents. Against such a disaster there is no more guarding than against the commission of more vulgar crimes; but when a government trembles for its existence, before the turbulence of popular commotion, it is reasonable to infer some radical defect in its organization. Men will rally around their institutions, as freely as they rally around any other cherished interest, when they merit their care, and there can be no surer sign of their hollowness than when the rulers seriously apprehend the breath of the mob. No nation ever exhibited more of this symptomatic terror, on all occasions of internal disturbance, than the pretending Republic of Venice. There was a never-ceasing and a natural tendency to dissolution, in her factious system, which was only resisted by the alertness of her aristocracy, and the political buttresses which their ingenuity had reared. Much was said of the venerable character of her policy, and of its consequent security, but it is in vain that selfishness contends with truth. Of all the fallacies with which man has attempted to gloss his expedients, there is none more evidently false than that which infers the duration of a social system, from the length of time it has already lasted. It would be quite as reasonable to affirm that the man of seventy has the same chances for life as the youth of fifteen, or that the inevitable fate of all things of mortal origin was not destruction."

Although Mao's age, the stooped, thin man looked Mao's elder by twenty years. But it was he, Cloudface, the one who had pouted and squirmed whenever disloyal remarks were made by his friends: Cloudface the drudge and scoffer.

"Ola, Cloudface. Do you still spend yourself in books and masturbation?"

"As usual, you exaggerate, Mao, just as you and your friends carried all thoughts to excess. Now your deeds have matched your most lunatic ideas. Who would have imagined that even your wildest schemes would have brought you to this marching at the head of a caravan of bandits."

"You are hurt, my old friend," Mao said placing his hand on the agitated scholar's shoulder. Regarding the man tenderly, Mao spoke, slowly, as if delivering one of his lectures to the troops. 'There is no frame permanent which is not founded on virtue, so there is no policy secure which is not bottomed on the good of the whole. Vulgar minds may control the concerns of the community so long as they are limited to vulgar views; but woe to the people who confide on great emergencies in any but the honest, the noble, the wise, and the philanthropic; for there is no security in success when the meanly artful control the occasional and providential events which regenerate a nation. More than half the misery which has defeated as well as disgraced civilization, proceeds from neglecting to use those great men that are always created by great occasions.'

"So say you, Mao. Yet you are still more in love with rhetoric than with individuals, still without humility—you have not changed, Mao, but today you have guns to make others believe as you do. 'This is always true of those men who have surrendered themselves to an overruling purpose. It does not so much impel them from within but grows incorporate with all that they think and feel, and finally converts them into little else save that one principle. When such begins to be the predicament, it is not cowardice, but wisdom, to avoid these victims. They have no heart, no sympathy, no reason, no conscience. They will keep no friend, unless he make himself the mirror of their purpose; they will smite and slay you, and trample your dead corpse under foot, all the more readily, if you take the first step with them and cannot take the second, and the third, and every other step of their terribly straight path. They have an idol, to which they consecrate themselves high priests, and deem it holy work to offer sacrifices of whatever is the most precious; and never once seem to suspect—so cunning had the devil been with them—that this false deity, in whose iron features, immitigable to all the rest of mankind, they see only benignity and love, is but the spectrum of the very priest himself projected upon the surrounding darkness. And the very higher and purer the original object, and the more unselfishly it may have been taken up, the slighter is the probability that they can be led to recognize the process by which godlike benevolence has been debased into all-devouring egotism.'

"What would you have, this nation chewed into scraps by foreigners until each of us beg in the streets for a cup of rice? Do you want the old way, scholars beaten, students shot, peasants and workers starved and humiliated? Is that better than my way, the way of all these marching men and those who believe in us? Cloudface, I have loved you in memory of those struggling days together, because those days were my youth. But now I have put away childish things and thoughts. Action with faith matters only. 'The good, the illuminated, sit apart from the rest, censuring their dullness and vices, as if they thought that by sitting very grand in their chairs, the very brokers, and congressmen would see the error of their ways and flock to them. But the good and the wise must learn to act, and carry salvation to the combatants and demagogues in the dusty arena below.' You are a halfway parasite: you have lingered while the Red Army drives forward, you have buried your feet in this stinking yellow clay while we hurtle to the clean future. You have a good heart, but your mind is a hotbed of timid ideas and paltry psychology."

As Mao finished speaking, a great grey cloud passed across the sun, bringing a green chill to the air. The wind gusted suddenly, and whisps of straw spun and careened about. Mao's peaked cap lofted nearly falling into the mud at his feet, but Cloudface scooped it up midair, and with a single swift sweep recrowned Mao's bare head. The two men faced each other silently while the wind fluttered their clothes like ragged banners. When the breeze finally slackened, Cloudface spoke.

'If anyone wishes to oppose the world, I suggest that he imitate Timon and retire to some wilderness where he may enjoy his wisdom alone.'

Mao tightened his gunbelt and silently joined the passing troops. From the height of a grassy knoll he wheeled about and thought he saw Cloudface scraping up the mud on which Mao had just stood.

From the outset the escape seemed doomed. The KMT bombed and machine-gunned the fleeing troops from the air, and Chiang mounted obstacle after obstacle in the Communist path. Eventually the Communists broke through, but this did not mean they were free: thousands of KMT troops pursued them; other thousands were sent to precede them at the Yangtze River, where Chiang was certain to crush them completely. The crossing points of the Yangtze were reinforced with men and weapons; boats and ferries were brought to the northern bank of the great river; and at all strategic points, blockades were raised.

"It was through an atmosphere of scalding heat and stifling dust that the brigade marched up the bluffs of Bayou Sara and over the rounded eminences which stretched on to Port Hudson. The perspiration which drenched the ragged uniforms and the pulverous soil which powdered them rapidly mixed into a muddy plaster; and the same plaster grimed the men's faces out of almost all semblance of humanity, except where the dust clung dry and grey to hair, beard, eyebrows, and eyelashes. So dense was the distressing cloud that it was impossible at times to see the length of a company. It seemed as if the men would go rabid with thirst, and drive the officers mad with their pleading to leave the ranks for water, a privilege not allowable to any great extent in an enemy's country. A lovely crystal

streamlet, running knee deep over clean yellow
sand, a charming contrast to black or brown
bayous with muddy and treacherous banks, was
forded by the feverish ranks with shouts and
laughter of childlike enjoyment. But it was
through volumes of burning yet lazy dust, soiling
and darkening the glory of sunset, that the brigade reached its appointed bivouac in a large
clearing, only two miles from the Rebel stronghold, though hidden from it by dense forest of
oaks, beeches, and magnolias."

The Red Army spent four months in Kweichow
trying to get out of the vast KMT trap. Many
battles and skirmishes were fought, during which
the KMT and warlord armies suffered great
losses; but the Communists were still faced with
crossing the Yangtze—either that or remain
many more months in the KMT bottleneck and
be slowly cut to pieces.

"Then shouting, 'Forward, men!' he ran down
to the palisade followed by twenty or thirty . . . .
"The assailing brigade, debouching from the
woods half a mile away from the Fort, had advanced in a wide front across the flat, losing
scarcely any men by the fire of the artillery, although many, shaken by the horrible screeching
of the hundred-pound shells, threw themselves
on the ground in the darkness or sought the frail
shelter of the scattered dwellings. Thus dimin-
ished in numbers and broken up by night and ob-
stacles and the differing speed of running men,
the brigade reached the Fort, not an organization
but a confused swarm, flowing along the edge of
the ditch to right and left in search of an en-
trance. There was a constant spattering of
flashes as individuals returned the steady fire of

the garrison; and the sharp clean whistle of round bullets and buckshot mingled in the thick warm air with the hoarse whiz of Miniés. Now and then an angry shout or wailing scream indicated that someone had been hit and mangled. The exhortations and oaths of the Rebel officers could be distinctly heard as they endeavored to restore order, to drive up stragglers, and to urge the mass forward. A few jumped or fell into the ditch and floundered there, unable to climb up the smooth facings of brickwork. Two or three hundred collected around the palisade which connected the northern front with the river, some lying down and waiting, and others firing at the woodwork or the neighboring ramparts, while a few determined ones tried to burst open the gate by main strength."

During The Long March, as has been said, the Communist ranks were often increased by peasants whose hatred of the warlords and the wealthy landlords had no previous outlet. Many joined simply because they were tired of their wretched lives, the young men especially, who wanted to escape ageless patterns of humiliation and starvation.

Bernard Lox, a man of many ailments, turned to his squat wife, Sadie, who was drinking tea out of a greasy *yahrzeit* glass. "It's a disaster, Sadie, a disaster. Our daughter falls in love with a *goy*. Who should think it would come to this. And me, an old man."

"Cheer up," Sadie said, washing the glass in the corroded and chipped porcelain sink as a cockroach danced on the faucet. "Cheer up, tomorrow we'll go by Klein's and buy a crate."

"A crate, Sadie?"

"A crate, Bernie."

"Oi, what should I want with a crate, me, an old old man, God should only know."

"A crate to sit *shivah* for Rebecca."

It was a good idea, he thought silently; a crate to sit *shivah*, so that God should know what misery they could endure now that Rebecca's ass had turned into a flower for the *goyim*.

With rare exceptions, these disaffected youths hardly understood the Reds' purposes and objectives, and of the more sophisticated ideology of the Communists they knew as much as an amoeba of astrophysics. Often these recruits thought themselves the hirelings of just another warlord and, as such, entitled to the rights of plunder and rape. For men like these, Mao had instituted the March and Study Program, an elementary course in Marxism taught by the more politically advanced members of the troops or, at times, by party members. At night, about a campfire, the new men sat in groups of seven, while the instructor lectured and read from works of Marx, Lenin, and Stalin.

Among the most difficult concepts for the new men to understand was that of equality of men and women. Dialectical and historical materialism, Theory of Value, Price and Profit, Imperialism, Contradiction—all these ideas were as simple as eating rice compared to the idea that a woman is a man's equal.

At first the new men laughed. Women equal to men? That was the best of everything! Women, whom one sold, however sorrowfully, during severe famines; women, the curse of a poor father, who would sooner drown a girl at birth than a litter of cats; women, who from childhood were taught to obey their fathers and husbands, beyond any wish or desire of their own; women, whom it cost less to sleep with than to buy a bowl of rice—women were equal to men?

With an especially difficult group, Mao himself led the course. The program began with the history of the origin and nature of the family from cave man to capitalism and went on to discuss the rôle of women under socialism. Theory was to be related to the practical concern of how women were to be treated in the present struggle, the revolutionary transition to socialism. And one night, standing before his group, Mao spoke the first rule of the Red Army with regard to women: "Soldiers of the Red Army, the Red Army soldier does not rape women!"

Mao continued to explain this unusual behavior: "Rape is a form of class aggression and is associated with other forms of class oppression, such as the exploitation of labor and the unjust taxes levied by landlords and warlords. Rape is committed by mercenary hordes, not a revolutionary army. Rape is a counterrevolutionary activity."

"Yes, boss," said one voice beyond the light of the small campfire, "but what are we to do without our wives and sweethearts?"

There were laughter and voices of approval. Even Mao had to laugh. But he immediately thought how fortunate he was in having his second wife with him, even if she was pregnant.

"Yes, yes, brothers, that is a fair question, but let me answer it by telling you the true history of the origin of the family and the institution of private property and the state."

"Tell us, tell us," cried one of the more historically minded comrades. The Mao, his handsome Lincolnesque face glowing in the firelight, began

to recite, in his lyrical, romantic voice, the history
of the origin of the family:

'Accordingly we have three principal forms of
marriage, which in the main correspond to the
three principal stages of human development.
For the period of savagery, the group marriage;
for barbarism, the pairing marriage; for civilization, monogamy supplemented by adultery and
prostitution. Between the pairing marriage and
monogamy there intervened, at the highest stage
of barbarism, the right of men to female slaves,
and polygamy.

'As our whole exposition has shown, the progress which manifests itself in this succession is
linked with the peculiarity that the sexual freedom of the group marriage is more and more
taken away from women, but not from men. And
in fact the group marriage continues to exist for
men actually up to the present time. What for a
woman is a crime drawing in its train grave legal
and social consequences, for a man is regarded
as honourable or at worst as a slight moral blem-
ish, easily tolerated. But the more the hetaerism
of antiquity is altered, in our age, by capitalist
commodity production and is adapted to this, the
more it is transformed into unconcealed prostitution, the more demoralizing are its effects. And
in fact it demoralizes men far more than women.
Prostitution degrades, among women, only the
unfortunate ones to whose lot it falls, and even
these not at all to the extent that is commonly
believed. On the other hand, it degrades the
character of the whole world of men. A long en-
gagement particularly is in nine cases out of ten
actually a preparatory school for marital in-
fidelity.

'We are now approaching a social revolution

in which the former economic foundations of monogamy will just as surely disappear as those of its complement, prostitution. Monogamy arose from the concentration of great riches in a single hand—that of the man—and from the need to bequeath these riches to the children of that man and not of any other. And for this purpose the monogamy of the woman was necessary, not that of the man, so that this monogamy of the woman did not at all stand in the way of open or concealed polygamy on the part of the man. The coming social revolution, however, through the transformation at least of the infinitely greater portion of permanent, heritable wealth—the means of production—into social property, will reduce this whole solicitude for inheritance to a minimum. If then monogamy came into being from economic causes, will it disappear when these causes disappear? It would be possible to answer, not without justice: far from disappearing, it will then on the contrary be fully realized for the first time. For with the transformation of the means of production into social property there will disappear also wage-labour, the proletariat, and therefore also the necessity for a certain—statistically calculable—number of women to surrender themselves for money. Prostitution disappears; monogamy, instead of collapsing, at last becomes a reality—even for men.

'The position of men is therefore in any case very much altered. But also the position of women, of *all* women, undergoes a significant change. With the transfer of the means of production into common ownership the individual family ceases to be the economic unit of society. Private housekeeping is transformed into a social industry. The care and education of children becomes a public affair; society looks after all children equally, whether they are legitimate or not. And this puts an end to the anxiety about the "consequences," which is now the most essential social—moral as well as economic—factor that deters a girl from giving herself without reluctance to the man she loves. Will that not be cause enough to bring about the gradual establishment of an unconstrained sexual intercourse, and with this also a more lenient public opinion in regard to maidenly honour and womanly shame. And finally, have we not seen that in the modern world monogamy and prostitution are, it is true, contradictions but inseparable contradictions, poles of the same social conditions? Can prostitution disappear without dragging monogamy down with it into the abyss?

'Here a new factor comes into play, a factor which, at the time when monogamy developed, existed at most in germ: individual sex-love.

'Before the Middle Ages there can be no question of individual sex-love. That personal beauty, intimate intercourse, sympathetic tastes, and so forth awakened the desire for sexual intercourse among people of opposite sexes; that both to men and to women it was not a matter of absolute indifference with whom they entered into this most intimate relationship—this goes without saying. But there is an infinite distance between that and our sex-love. Throughout the whole ancient world marriages were arranged by the parents for the partners, and the latter were easily reconciled. The little portion of marital love known to antiquity is not any subjective inclination but an objective duty; not a ground but a correlative of marriage. Love relationships in the modern sense only make their appearance in antiquity outside of official society. The shepherds of whose joys and sorrows in love Theocritus and

Moschus sing, the Daphnis and Chloe of Longos, were simple slaves who had no share in the State, the free citizens' sphere of life. Apart from slaves we find love affairs only as products of the disintegration of the old world in its decline, and with women who also stood outside official society, with hetaerae, that is, with "barbarians" or freed slaves: in Athens from the eve of its ruin onwards, in Rome at the time of the Caesars. If love affairs really developed between free men and women citizens, it was only through adultery. And to the classical love poet of antiquity, old Anakreon, sex-love in our sense was of so little concern that even the sex of the loved one was a matter of absolute indifference to him.

'Our sex-love is essentially different from the simple sexual desire, the Eros, of the ancients. In the first place, it presupposes that the love is reciprocated by the loved one; to this extent the woman stands on the same footing as the man, while in the Eros of antiquity she was by no means always asked. Secondly, our sex-love has a degree of intensity and duration which makes both lovers feel that non-possession and separation are a very great, if not the greatest, misfortune. In order to ensure mutual possession they risk high stakes, even staking their lives—a thing which in antiquity happened only in adultery. And finally a new moral standard arises by which sexual intercourse is judged; we not only ask whether it was within the marriage tie, but also whether it sprang from love and reciprocated love or not. Of course this new standard has fared no better in feudal or bourgeois practice than any other moral standard—it is simply ignored. But also it fares no worse. It is recognized to the same extent as previous standards—in theory, on paper. And at present it can ask no more than this.

'At the point where antiquity ended its progress towards sex-love, the Middle Ages took it up —in adultery. We have already spoken of the knightly love which gave rise to the songs. From this love, urging violation of the marriage tie, to the love which is to be the foundation of marriage, is still a long road, and this road was never fully traversed by the knights. Even when we pass from the frivolous Latin race to the virtuous Germans, we find in the *Nibelungenlied* that although in her heart Kriemhild is not less in love with Siegfried than he is with her, when Gunther tells her that he has promised her to a knight whom he does not name, she simply answers: "You have no need to ask me; as you bid me, so will I ever be; the man whom you, lord, give me to wed, that man will I gladly take in troth." It does not even enter her head that her love can in any way come into consideration in this matter. Gunther asks for Brünhild, Etzel for Kriemhild, although they have never seen each other; the same is true of the suit of Gutrun Sigebant of Ireland for the Norwegian Ute, of Hetel of Hegelingen's suit for Hilde of Ireland; and finally of Siegfried of Morland, Hartmut of Ormanien and Herwig of Zeeland, in their suit for Gutrun—and in this case for the first time it happens that Gutrun voluntarily decides in favour of the last-named of the three. As a rule the young prince's bride is selected by his parents, if they are still living, and if not, by the prince himself on the advice of the great feudal lords, whose views in all cases carry considerable weight. And it cannot be otherwise. For the knight or baron, as the head of the land himself, marriage is a political act, an occasion for the extension of power through new alliances; the interest of the *house* must be decisive, not the wishes of the individual. In such circumstances how can love reach the position in which it has the decisive say in marriage?

'The same held good for the guild member in the towns of the Middle Ages. The privileges protecting him, the clauses of the guild charters, the artificial lines of demarcation which legally cut him off, both from the other guilds, and from other members of his own guild and from his own journeymen and apprentices, already sufficiently narrowed down the circle within which he might select a suitable spouse. And in that complicated system it was certainly not his individual fancy but the interests of the family which decided who was the most suitable spouse within that circle.

'In the infinitely greater majority of cases, therefore, marriage remained, up to the close of the Middle Ages, what it had been from the very beginning—a matter which the partners did not decide. In the earliest stages men and women were already married when they came into the world—married to an entire group of the opposite sex. In the later forms of group marriage probably similar relations existed, but within continually contracting groups. In the pairing marriage it was customary for the mothers to arrange the marriages of their children; here too the decisive considerations are the new ties of kinship which can win for the young couple a stronger position in the gens and tribe. And when, with the predominance of private over communal property and the growing concern for inheritance, patriarchy and monogamy came to dominate, marriage then became completely dependent on economic considerations. The *form* of marriage by purchase disappeared, but the practice itself came to be more and more consistently applied, so that not only the woman but also the man acquired a price—based not on his personal characteristics but on his property. From the very beginning the conception that the mutual inclination of the contracting parties should be the ground, outweighing all others, for the marriage was completely unheard of in the practice of the ruling classes. Anything of this sort occurred at best in romance, or—among the oppressed classes, who did not count.

'Such was the state of things which capitalist production found in existence when, following the epoch of geographical discoveries, it set out to conquer the world through trade and manufacture. It might have assumed that this mode of marriage suited it exceptionally well; and such was the case. And yet—the irony of history knows no limit—it was capitalist production which was destined to make the decisive breach in this mode of marriage. By transforming everything into commodities, it destroyed all inherited, traditional relationships, it set up, in place of time-honoured custom and historical right, purchase and sale and "free" contract. The English jurist H. S. Maine thought he had made an immense discovery when he stated that our whole progress as compared with former epochs consisted in the fact that we had passed from status to contract, from inherited and traditional conditions to those brought into being by voluntary contract—a statement which, in so far as it is correct, was already, as a matter of fact, contained in *The Communist Manifesto.*

'The making of contracts, however, requires people who can freely dispose of their persons, actions, and possessions, and meet each other on the basis of equal rights. It was precisely the creations of these "free" and "equal" people that was one of the principal functions of capitalist society. And although at first it happened only in a half-conscious way, and moreover disguised in religious wrappings, by the time of the Lutheran and Calvinistic Reformation it was an established principle that man is only fully responsible for his actions when he acts with complete freedom of will, and that it is a moral obligation to resist all coercion to an immoral act. But how did this fit in with former practice in the arrangement of marriages? According to the bourgeois conception, marriage was a contract, a juridical matter, and indeed the most important of all contracts, because it disposed of the body and mind of the two human beings for the period of their life. It is true that at that time, from a formal standpoint, it was entered into voluntarily; it could not be completed without the assent of the persons concerned. But everyone knew only too well how this assent was obtained, and who were the real contracting parties to the marriage. But if real freedom of decision was required for all other contracts, why not also in this one? Had not the two young people who were to be united in marriage also the right to dispose freely of themselves, of their body and its organs? Had not sex-love come into fashion through the knights, and, in contrast to the adulterous love of the age of chivalry, was not the love of one's own spouse its proper bourgeois form? And if it was the duty of married people to love each other, was it not equally the duty of lovers to marry each other and no one else? Was not the right of lovers superior to the right of parents, relatives and other traditional marriage brokers and agents? If the right of free personal investigation made its way unchecked into the church and religion, how could it stand still in face of the older generation's intolerable claim to dispose over the body, soul, property, weal and woe of young persons?

'These questions had to be raised at a period which loosened all the old ties of society and shattered all inherited conceptions. The world had suddenly become almost ten times bigger; instead of a quadrant of a hemisphere, the whole globe now lay before the eyes of the West Europeans, who hastened to take possession of the other seven quadrants. And along with the old narrow barriers of their native land, the thousand-year-old barriers of mediaeval conventional thought were also broken down. An infinitely wider horizon opened out before both the outward and the inward gaze of man. What mattered the prospects offered by respectability, or the honourable guild privileges inherited through generations, to the young man tempted by the wealth of India, the gold and silver mines of Mexico and Potosis? It was the knight-errant period of the bourgeoisie; it had too its romance and its amorous enthusiasms, but on a bourgeois footing, and in the last analysis, with bourgeois aims.

'So it came about that the rising bourgeoisie, especially in the Protestant countries where existing institutions were most severely shaken, more and more came to recognize freedom of contract also in marriage, and developed it in the way described above. Marriage remained class marriage, but a certain degree of free choice within the class was allowed to the partners. And on paper, in ethical theory and poetic description, nothing was more firmly established than that every marriage is immoral which does not rest on mutual sex-love and really free contract between husband and wife. In a word, the love-marriage was proclaimed as a human right, and indeed not only as *droit de l'homme,* but even by way of exception as *droit de la femme.*

'This human right, however, differed in one respect from all other so-called human rights. While the latter, in practice, remained restricted to the ruling class, the bourgeoisie, and were directly or indirectly curtailed for the oppressed class, the proletariat, in the case of the former the irony of history once more lived up to its reputation. The ruling class remained dominated by the familiar economic influences, and therefore only in exceptional cases provided instances of really freely contracted marriages, while these, as we have seen, were the rule among the oppressed class.

'Full freedom of marriage can therefore only become generally established when the abolition of capitalist production and of the property relations created by it has done away with all the economic considerations which still exert such powerful influence on the choice of a spouse. For then no motive other than mutual affection will be left.'

When Mao finished his monologue, he wiped his forehead with his red hankie and drank a mouthful of warm water from his canteen.

"Now, any questions, men?"

Only the historically minded comrade, one of Mao's distant cousins, raising himself on his elbow and opening his leaden eyes, replied: "This is most enlightening, comrade Mao. Perhaps now you will explain the proper course of behavior for the Red Army soldier toward women when he marches through unfamiliar villages."

"That is a good question. But it is late, and we must rest our weary bodies for the morning's

hard march." And Mao stumbled off into the
rising rosy dawn, determined to answer that
question the next evening.

As we have heard, Mao was an astute commentator on the woman question. Mao knew the issue from both theory and practice. He had known the old, feudal way of marriage—his parents had married him off when he was fourteen to the teenage daughter of another peasant, a marriage which Mao rejected—as well as modern romantic love.

Mao's first romance occurred when he was a revolutionary student in Peiping. The young man fell in love with his teacher's daughter, Yang K'ai-hui, a chaste, virtuous, passionate girl, and married her in 1921. From all reports they were a happy pair who loved one another, the revolution, and their son. Several years later, whatever the reason, Mao began an affair with an eighteen-year-old girl, Ho Tze-nein, with whom he was to have five children. In 1930, Mao's legitimate wife was executed by the KMT after the failure of the Red attack on Ch'angsha.

A photo of Mao with his second wife, Ho Tze-nein, taken during The Long March, shows them smiling and glowing in an ascetic way. Ho Tze-nein was a slender, spirited woman, and in her blue uniform and jaunty worker's cap she seemed Mao's counterpart — an ideal comrade and lover. Mao was known to have said to a comrade: "Some day perhaps Ho Tze-nein and I will be written about. It will be a new story of love, a new culture myth of Communist love, as Shakespeare's Antony and Cleopatra are of the old feudal, Renaissance, capitalist heartbreak love. What, after all, was Antony and Cleopatra's love but the decadent love of sex and power? She loved Antony's power, which she translated into sexual love; he loved her sexually, which he translated into power, giving her kingdoms, setting her up against her brother as ruler of the Nile. Cleopatra deserted Antony when she thought he had lost power. That is true Western capitalist love: Shakespeare understood it and did not lie. Those two did not love one another, they were only mad for each other's personification—she was Egypt and he, Rome. When they made love at night the earth shook—as their soldiers reported—because they were geographies in collision, not humans in embrace."

All of Mao's comrades admired the pair, and young revolutionaries took them as models to emulate: their relationship was not only a triumph of love but also a victory of the new politics. Here was the pattern for the new socialist marriage, no more the subservience of the woman and the ruthless domination of the man, no more the old-styled fearful, cowering woman. Ho Tze-nein was one of the thirty-five women on The Long March, and she was pregnant for part of the journey. Not only did she suffer the ordeal of carrying a child during the march but she also was wounded by bomb fragmentation. Some years later while she was away in Moscow for medical treatment, Mao divorced her and married the actress Lan-p'ing, whose ambience had been, in contrast to Mao's background, exotic, steeped, as it were, in the culture of the city and the theatre. Some suspect that Mao was mad for Lan-p'ing's lilac painted toenails, a trick she picked up in Shanghai, 1933.

Theory and proscription concerning the individual's sexual behavior perhaps did have the function of enlightening and regulating the individual soldier's actions, yet most of the sexual practices of the Red Army were never codified nor written into social doctrine but arose out of the particular conditions of The Long March, chief among which was the need for a rapid egress from one's sexual partner in the event of an unexpected enemy attack by land or air.

A favorite position during intercourse, then, was the man-on-bottom, woman-sitting-on-top formation, a desirable attitude for several reasons. For one, the soldier could keep his rifle at his side, and in the event of a rush attack, he could shoot from a sitting-up position, weapon at his hip, while the woman dashed away for cover. From this position, too, the soldier could easily shoot straight up at a plane overhead. For another reason, this position reflected the new revolutionary spirit: the woman was given the chance to be on top for a while. And in this posture the soldier could readily drop off to sleep after making love, no small consideration for a man on the march the whole day.

Usually, however, the soldiers were too tired to think of sex. After a day's march over hills and dales and steep roads and narrow, rocky trails, it was enough to plunk down at night and try to find a dry spot to sleep on. Under such conditions it was all a man could do to manage a quick jerk-off under the dewy milk-stars faraway.

Take a stanza. Any of several. The fecund succession of images tumbles, cascades in an interlocking, chain-reacting, ever-widening yet self-echoing reverberation of referential and metaphorical assertions and postures. Line four of stanza three threatens to bound, to mutiny against the agitation of the driving anapests of line three, but in its periodic formation, the line rescues itself from collapse two beats away from the pronounced spondee of the verb. But enough of this impressionistic investigation. Let us investigate more empirical tests of the stanza.

Imagery gives not only texture to the poem but functions as the discrete locus of the work, the controlling design which reveals the intent (subconsciously rendered or purposefully ordered), beyond the meaning or implications of the narrative line of the work.

In this poem images of synesthesia and oxymoron decidedly mould meaning, lending to the work a certain hermetic, neo-Platonic tone and implication. These images undercut one another not in *effect* but in sense, so that the world of the poem is in imagistic stasis, and the poem itself is given an immutable and dynamic locus: permanency and change unite to form a synthesis at once inexplicable and emotionally logical. To leave off the linguistic system of the poem for a moment is to enter into that ineffable realm of enigma and ambiguity, of intellectual and transcendental excitation terminating in rest and harmony; ganglia and synapses lapse into sentient passivity, the mind and body assume a state of aesthetic grace.

Few moments in life convey the sense of life lived as well as that given by a poem in its perfect condition: no adventure, no possession, no human relationship equals the experience given by a poem in its perfect manifestation. In this sense, each perfect poem is a challenge and assault to Nature, since it declares man's self-sufficiency from it. This is an old argument, you say, another form of hedonism dressed in new linguistic trappings, a turn and escape from the concerns of life, from the jail of body functions, from aching feet and going bald, from menopause and impotence and bad breath, from the amatory itch. A nostrum, you say, for recluses and timids, for constipated queers and androgynous mama's boys. Say what you will, say even worse but, in truth, poetry is revolution without bloodshed; it is a mantle of stars without the cold of interstellar space; the sea without its preying sharks; a sand desert made of water crystals. I digress.

"Hymn to a Cockroach" is surely one of the major poems of this century; and in terms of literary tradition, it ranks among the master artifacts of transcendental mythology, bordering between the metaphysical poetry of the seventeenth century and the baroque poetry of Marino. The cockroach belongs in the bestiary that includes Faulkner's sapient bear and Melville's ontological whale. The "Hymn" is at once prayer and curse, invective and eulogy, a Manichean forecast and an Emersonian dissertation—some critics have claimed that the poem had predicted the major holocausts of the modern age, others have seen in it the message of salvation for our declining civilization.

The "Hymn," however, belongs, in theme and chronology, beside the longer "Cockroach in the Rose Garden," an amalgam of Surrealist and Cubist iconography (the obvious sources being Max Ernst, Marcel Duchamp, René Magritte, Juan Gris, Braque, and Picasso) and a Yeats-Eliot-Pound ambience of discord and synthesis. Nonetheless, the diction and rhythms of "Cockroach in a Rose Garden" bear heavily on the discoveries of William Carlos Williams and Charles Olson, and, ultimately, on Hopkins's Sprung Rhythm, and the long line of Whitman's 1855 *Leaves of Grass* find their echoes in this magnificent *mélange*.

I should not neglect, too, the debt to popular

cinema. The films of Charlie Chaplin are as important to these poems as are the influences of Anglo-Saxon, Decadent, and eighteenth-century (Pope) English verse. Charlie, in his pathetic picaresque adventures strongly resembles the strutting and crafty innocence of our poet's cockroach—both innocent persona and archetypal life-force image.

Chaplin may be considered the classical cinematic source, but the poet leans no less heavily on the more contemporary films of Sam Fuller *(Shock Corridor)*, Vincent Minnelli *(Two Weeks in Another Town)*, John Ford (of the *Stagecoach* period), and the early Jerry Lewis films, especially *Nutty Professor* and *The Caddy*. No account of

In May, 1935, Mao attempted a diversionary manoeuvre, sending what seemed his entire force through Yunnan (where the Chinese border joins Burma and Indo-China) and on to its capital, Yunnanfu. Convinced that Mao was pressing on to Yunnanfu, Chaing sent his planes and a great portion of his troops there to cut the Reds off. But Mao was actually moving westward, in the hope of crossing the Yangtze at the Lengkai slip; his avant-garde marched day and night trying to find an opening, a crossing point for the hard-pressed troops following them.

Dusk. A sickle moon. Dry snow on moundlike hills. Campfires glowing like red coals on the darkening snowfield. Machine guns planted side by side in clumps of three like little rows of stunted fir trees. The flaps of Mao's tent smack.

Steam rising from kettles of boiling rice. Steam from the hot manure of tethered horses and mules strung along the picket line. Mao's wife brings him a pot of tea. She resembles an ordinary quilted foot soldier and Mao does not recognize her. He continues to look up at the stars and the moon and then again at the campfires and the men and the animals. He drinks the tea slowly.

"Are you wistful, Mao?"

"No, my dear. I'm thinking of blackbirds."

"Any kind especially?"

"Three of them in a tree."

"What else?"

"Urns and empty glass jars."

"How would they look in this field?"

"Like a Beethoven string quartet."

"Or a Cézanne still life?"

"Like that too."

Mao's wife sighs. "Come to bed, my sweet man; you need to dream."

"Not tonight. Tonight I would like to love you alone."

"Oh! Mao, the world is too tired for that."

"We must stir it to life then. The sexual act is a revolutionary act."

"True, Mao. To embrace is to help heal the world's wounds."

"I have thought so too, more so now that I begin to sense that 'Merely skimming the surface of life, I know nothing, by my own experience, of its deep warm realities. I have achieved none of these objects which the instinct of mankind especially prompts them to pursue, and the accomplishment of which must therefore beget a native satisfaction. The truly wise, after all their speculations, will be led into the common path, and, in homage to the human nature that pervades them, will gather gold, and till the earth, and set out trees, and build a house.'

"The campfire is your hearth, the revolution your home, my dear husband."

"No, the revolution is my poem."

"Well, then?"

"Something is wrong with the imagery."

"What else?"

"The structure is too random."

"Revise after you have completed it."

"It will cease to exist when finished."

"Then there is nothing to do now but to go to bed."

Arm in arm they shuffled to their tent. Mao remembered that he had left a blue porcelain teacup by the campfire but he was too tired to retrieve it. As he passed off to sleep, he thought he would leave it there in the snow, by the fire, under the sky, stars, and moon.

One evening, Mao's vanguard, disguised in KMT uniforms, casually walked into the Chou P'ing fort and quickly, silently overpowered the astonished garrison. Although the garrison had not expected the Reds, thinking the main force some three days away and marching in an entirely different direction, they had taken the precaution of sending all their boats to the garrison at the opposite bank. The Communists, however, found a small dinghy the soldiers had overlooked, and with a captive officer at the bow, several Reds crossed over. In one rush the Reds captured the dozing KMT guards.

The following morning, when Mao and the troops arrived, there were six large boats ready to ferry them across. The Communists worked feverishly to get everyone over before Chiang's forces could reach and destroy the divided troops. The KMT army arrived two days after the last boat touched the north shore. Chiang's troops could not find one boat, one log — the Communists had burned everything that could float—and they had to march over one hundred miles to another crossing point. By that time, the Communists were driving to the Tatu, the last major river that had to be crossed before they could be safe from the threat of KMT entrapment. In all probability, Chiang realized that if the Reds were not stopped at the Tatu, it would be extremely difficult to destroy them later, when they would be in regions not dominated by the KMT and its allies: Chiang would have to send his troops further and further away from central sources of supplies and weapons. Therefore, Chiang concentrated all his air and land power in the Tatu River campaign.

Not long after the decisive withdrawal from the Kiangsi base in January, 1935, the Communists held a conference to decide on the leadership of the party and its policy. The outcome of the meeting was significant to the course of The Long March. For one, Mao was given leadership of the party and, perhaps more importantly in terms of the immediate situation, the party decided that the reason for the withdrawal from Kiangsi was primarily to fight the Japanese in the north, and the slogan under which Mao led The Long March became: "Drive north to fight the Japanese."

The slogan served two strategic functions: it gave Mao a rationale for the drive north, turning an escape into an attack, and with the impetus of a war against a foreign invader it offered the

Red Army a unity stronger than ever before. With the emphasis on a national struggle against a common enemy, Mao was able to attract the good will of much of the peasantry and even some of the hostile warlords through whose territories he would have to pass. Many pro-Chiang soldiers and officers, especially in Manchuria, joined the Reds won over by Mao's insistence that all Chinese must unite to repel the invaders before China could resolve its internal differences.

Whee. Whee. Pres brought the car round the corner in a mad tragic sort of screech and it made me think how in my less hip student days when me and Fox roamed the beat streets (that was in 1943 when Lou Bell and Andy Green sang their last blueslovepoem before making it to the neverheardofagain volcanos of Mexico) digging the chicks with their short skirts and cute knee dimples it made my heart sink and Fox said let's take the Ferry to saintly Staten Island and groove with the sunrise over New York.

With the renewed purpose of the fight against the Japanese and with the threat of annihilation waiting for them should they fail at the Tatu, the Communists intensified their efforts to reach and cross the huge swift river.

On a knoll some yards off the path where the file of troops passed with a dull clanking of pots and pans and light artillery, Mao glimpsed a pyramidical clump of tattered rags and animal skins. It moved, and Mao, pistol in hand, cautiously walked toward the pile. It took some while for Mao to realize that the form covered with nettles and leaves was a man. With his long hair and beard matted with flies and dead ants, pollen and weeds, and with what was visible of his face weathered like the soil and rock on which he sat, it was impossible to tell the man's age.

"How are you, old one?"

"Well, young soldier."

Some crows flew down on the man's shoulders and pecked at the vermin in his hair. Mao wondered what to say next.

"Do my troops disturb you?"

"No."

"Would you like some water?"

"Thank you, no. I had some last week."

Mao grew irritated. "You're a very holy fellow, eh!" The man did not respond but regarded Mao as if he were an old familiar tree.

"I'm a revolutionary," Mao declared, feeling foolish the moment he spoke the words. Wincing, the man gently removed a worm that had been burrowing into his ear and fed it to the crows.

"Yes, so you are, Mao."

"My men and I will change the old ways," Mao said, pointing to the line of passing soldiers and weapons.

'I have seen how the foundations of the world are laid, and I have not the least doubt that it will stand a good while.'

"The foundations of this world are rotten and will crumble with our strong push."

'Tell me that the rivers are drying up, or the genus pine dying out in the country and I might attend.'

"You have had your head up so long in the sky that you do not see your feet wading in shit."

'Your scheme must be the framework of the universe; all other schemes will soon be ruins.'

"Let's first make revolution, then fly to heaven together."

"First come to heaven with me and you shall have made your revolution."

"What? To sit beside you like a heap of clothed dung and fancy myself better than the suffering world? You are my worst enemy," Mao shouted. "You and your kind would make us eat garbage and call it honey."

"Whatever you eat, Mao, you will always be hungry." Mao stamped his foot. What could he do to wake this man from his dream?

"Join us and I shall make you a commander of an army."

"Why?"

"I like your style."

'I would give all the wealth of the world, and all the deeds of all the heroes, for one true vision.'

"And you must have many of them, living as you do. Give me a vision and I will join you," Mao said contemptuously.

"Is that all, one vision?"

"Yes."

"Remove your shoes."

Mao sloughed off his mud-caked boots and hitched up his gun belt.

"Sit down and look at your feet."

"What is there to see?" Mao asked after a moment. "Dirt, sweat, bunions?"

"What else?"

"Skin, nails."

"Else?"

"Nothing."

"Good, your vision is complete."

"You pompous old fake," Mao hissed, sud-

denly feeling naked without his shoes, humiliated.

The crows flew up from the old man's shoulders and circled Mao's head. He became uneasy,
and, with shoes in hand, he silently rejoined his
troops. At last look, Mao saw the old man exam-
ining his own feet, which from the distance
seemed roots of young trees.

The Reds abruptly decided to shift course and
pushed through into the hostile Lololand, a
region inhabited by a fierce tribe, the Lolos,
whom the Chinese had never completely sub-
jugated. The reason was that the Lolos lived in
a densely forested and mountainous terrain,
where the Reds, if they had the cooperation of
the tribesmen, could temporarily evade the KMT
reconaissance and fighter planes that bombed
and machine-gunned them every day and kept
an accurate chart of their progress to the Tatu.
Fortunately for the Communists, one of their
officers, Commander Lin Pei-ch'eng, was familiar with the Lolos and even spoke their dia-
lect. Many years before he had lived among them
with his beautiful Lolo bride, "She who eats
bamboo shoots with chestnuts," a daughter of a
powerful chieftain. Shortly after, she had died in
childbirth, and the young husband had left the
tribe to join the revolution under Sun Yat-sen.
When the Red troops entered the Lolo territory,
Lin was first in a scouting party that made contact with the tribesmen. The Lolos recognized
him and they instantly began speaking of mutual
friends and relatives in a nearby village.

Presently a parley was held among Lolo chiefs

and the army commanders. After much feasting and exchanges of gifts—one of the sewing machines borne by the Communists was planted in a chief's sleeping room where it remained as a symbol of Lolo-Red friendship—Mao explained that, like the Lolos, the Reds too were persecuted by bad Chinese, and that the Reds wanted to free all of China from these Chinese, after which the Lolos would have their independence guaranteed. Negotiations were advanced considerably when several of Mao's officers offered to marry Lolo widows and oldish spinsters and to take them along on their march north.

In this way the Lolos and the Reds became allies; many young Lolo warriors accompanied and guided the troops through the dense forest to the Tatu. And as the KMT pilots vainly searched for them, a vanguard battalion led by Lin Piao raced ahead of the army. After several days of forced marching over narrow mountain passes, the vanguard arrived, unspotted, at the river town of An Jen Ch'ang. From high above the river the Lolo scouts and the Red unit could see two ferries beyond their reach on the north bank. They almost shouted in despair. Suddenly, one of the youngest soldiers pointed to the bank directly below them: there, half-concealed by the overhanging ferry slip, was a boat large enough to hold eight men. Perhaps it was a trap, an experienced fighter suggested as they discussed the means of attacking the drowsy town below. It was decided to send into town five men wearing KMT uniforms, as they had done during the attack at the Yangtze, while the rest of the band hid in the town margin waiting for word of the situation. The men embraced in a comradely hug of farewell; tears were shed even by the most grizzled Long Marchers.

The five entered the town unobtrusively, pretending to be stragglers on patrol. It was noon. Even the bony dogs were sleeping. The ferry ship was unguarded. On signal, the rest entered the town, captured the barracks and their commander, who was busy playing *mah-jong* with his wife. The wife was dressed in her finest silks and lace—she had been waiting to leave the town at three that afternoon to go to her sister's wedding. The ferry had been left behind for that purpose. Not believing that the Reds were anywhere in the vicinity, the commander had disobeyed orders in not sending all the boats to the north bank. Three days after the town's capture, the commander shot himself rather than face Chiang's wrath.

A runner was immediately dispatched to the main troops, while the unit crossed over and seized the remaining ferries. Only two lives were lost in the entire venture, and many KMT arms were added to the Reds' meager supplies.

With three ferries continuously plying the river, many men were quickly brought to the safety of the north bank. But two problems were pressing the Reds: they had been located, and the KMT planes were now bombing them incessantly, and Chiang's troops were rushing to encircle them. Meanwhile, the May rains had flooded and swollen the river, and the current was rushing at an increased rate daily. Each day progress across grew more difficult. On the third day only eight crossings were made, and one boatload was swamped, with the loss of sixty soldiers. It was apparent that Chiang's troops would arrive before all the Reds were safely across and pounce when they were divided, crushing them all the more easily.

The only other crossing point within safe distance was at the iron suspension bridge at Tatu, called Lin Ting Chiao, some two hundred miles further up river. To get to the Lin Ting Chiao was itself a feat . . . the bridge spanned an immensely high, narrow gorge, whose approach had to be made almost in single file along tortuous mountain paths. If the bridge could be reached in time, there was still no certainty that it could be crossed, since only a handful of men on the opposite side could hold off an army for weeks— more than enough time for Chiang to arrive and slaughter the Reds trapped in the bare mountain slopes. The risk had to be taken, nevertheless. One hundred men with Lolo scouts ran and forced-marched for two days and nights, sleeping only a few hours and eating cold rice while on the run.

"A short march brought them to the foot of the mountain, but its steep and cragged sides almost discouraged hope. The only chance of scaling it was by broken masses of rock, piled one upon another, which formed a succession of crags, reaching nearly to the summit. Up these they wrought their way with indescribable difficulty and peril, in a zigzag course, climbing from rock to rock, and helping their horses up after them, which scrambled among the crags like mountain goats, now and then dislodging some huge stone, which, the moment they had left it, would roll down the mountain, crashing and rebounding with terrific din. It was some time after dark before they reached a kind of platform on the summit of the mountain, where they could venture to encamp. The winds, which swept this naked height, had whirled all the snow into the valley beneath, so that the horses found tolerable winter pasturage on the dry grass which remained exposed. The travellers, though hungry in the extreme, were fain to make a very frugal supper; for they saw their journey was likely to be prolonged much beyond the anticipated term.

"In fact, on the following day they discerned that, although already at a great elevation, they were only as yet upon the shoulder of the mountain. It proved to be a great sierra, or ridge, of immense height, running parallel to the course of the river, swelling by degrees to lofty peaks, but the outline gashed by deep and precipitous ravines. This, in fact, was a part of the chain of Blue Mountains, in which the first adventurers to Astoria experienced such hardship.

"We will not pretend to accompany the travellers step by step in this tremendous mountain scramble, into which they had unconsciously betrayed themselves. Day after day did their toil continue; peak after peak had they to traverse, struggling with difficulties and hardships known only to the mountain trapper. As their course lay north, they had to ascend the southern faces of the heights, where the sun had melted the snow, so as to render the ascent wet and slippery, and to keep both men and horses continually on the strain; while on the northern sides, the snow lay in such heavy masses that it was necessary to beat a track, down which the horses might be led. Every now and then, also, their way was impeded by tall and numerous pines, some of which had fallen, and lay in every direction.

"In the midst of these toils and hardships their provisions gave out. For three days they were without food, and so reduced that they could scarcely drag themselves along. At length one of the mules, being about to give out from fatigue and famine, they hastened to dispatch him. Husbanding this miserable supply, they dried the flesh, and for three days subsisted upon the nutriment extracted from the bones. As to the meat, it was packed and preserved as long as they could do without it, not knowing how long they might remain bewildered in these desolate regions."

Meanwhile, as another vanguard of 10,000 men pushed forward along both sides of the river, the Red Army pulled behind. Each soldier knew that the outcome at the Tatu bridge might well decide the future of the entire Communist movement in China.

Then it rained hard on the dead wet leaves. And you knew that if you said it all truly there would be enough there for a long time. Enough of the olives and Baked Alaska when the air conditioner blew at you hard in the fine little room behind the zinc of the bar at Sardi's. Nick stood up and hit the waiter hard just below the temple. The man went down. The cool red borscht flew from his hands and spilled into rivulets. Three waiters came at us and you put the empty champagne bottle to your cheek and popped them down as they moved fast coming at you with a sudden rush. Hi ho, said Mary, as you counted the saucers and left a tip although you were poor. If it were true enough it would all be there. It would all be there if you said it truly.

On the second day the Communist troops on the northern bank fell behind exhausted; soldiers wept with fatigue and anguish, their wails could be heard far across the gorge and high above on the jagged cliffs. On the third day the troops advancing on the southern bank spotted a division of Chiang's men on the opposite shore. The two armies lined along the banks and cliffs shouting and cursing one another and shooting off a few hundred rounds of random shots. The KMT troops were pressing ahead to reinforce the garrison at the Tatu bridge, and they too knew the consequence of their victory or failure.

Oblivious of the action in the rear, what remained of the hundred scouts (several had fallen to their death in the stony passes and a few hearts had burst from exhaustion) reached the bridge to find the planks across it had been removed. The iron bridge swayed before them like some ancient ribald skeleton.

In the anguished art of Hans Haddock, the purely gestural utterances—the slide, skid, glide, and quirky doodles on the painting skin—react in obedient suspension with the more formal rhetorical devices of the artist's tortured craft. In every resonant slide of the gestural track lies the secret of the void—a void Haddock looked into during the bitter years of 1950 to 1955 when, alone, impoverished, and ill from too much drinking and too many ruinous love affairs, he broke through every aesthetic and personal barrier to revivify the moribund and ossified painting of his generation. Haddock struck deep down to the rich sources of art by tapping the pure wells of his own psyche—wells filled with the violence and torment only a man of his commitment and integrity could spring.

In the five years of Haddock's major phase, there evolved an archetypal painting and painting behavior (how else shall we designate a process so allied to life style?) which bears discussion. His large painting "Moondance for the Bird" is an eulogistic elegy for the great jazz musician who trumpeted his soul across the vast wastes of the grey American 1950's, with its politics of banality and plastic sexuality. Haddock responded to that dead-pan sterility and the death of his friend with a painting glutted with the texture of despair. The all-over gookie surface bathed the more sedate areas of paint skin, giving the generous field a tortured, writhing appearance. At no point can the plane be deciphered from the field, so total was Haddock's commitment to the lay-down impasto of the embattered arena. And, as if the intensity of his anguish had correspondence in hot colors, an arbitrariness with open-ended allowances for improvisation, barbaric reds and molten oranges stream in all the discord of passionate randomness and premeditated accident.

"Moondance for a Bird," wrote Haddock to Jennifer Squibb, Springs, L. I., in the winter of 1952, "was painted some hours after you left my studio on 11th Street. I was feeling blue. You were gone. I thought forever. Maybe I'd go down to the Cedar and see Franz and Bill and Jack and Hans, and have a few beers and laughs, I reflected. But what was the use of being with the boys, when it was you I really wanted? So, I put up some coffee and pulled on another sweater —you had told me you would never shack up with me until I got a better heater. You were right, my hands and teeth were ice and the paintbrushes were frozen brittle. Then I got the heebie-jeebies from being all alone in that cold, dark loft with its damp concrete floor. I spun a disc—the first one on the pile near the bed. It was Bird. I remember how you flipped your tits into your sexy bra just before you left, and I was getting crazy to mush you up again. I thought of phoning you but I was too tired and cold to go through the whole thing of walking down to the corner in the slush and coming back up again after a few words to you. And who knows, maybe we'd fight again. And you can be the world's worst bitch on the phone when you want. So I stayed and looked at the canvas tacked on the wall. That big stupid hunk of material. Sweet Mama! I wanted to fuck it. You know what I mean."

Haddock, as this letter reveals, was in despair: Bird's plaintive wail stirred him, as though by trance, to make plastic all that Bird had cried through his horn. All of the Bird's riffs and toots and long silky slides were metamorphosed into Haddock's skirmishes with the brute, raw (unprimed) canvas—like the great white whale whom he must pursue and attack to the ultimate, annihilating brush swipe.

The band decided to attempt to capture the bridge, assuming that the wooden planks were being stored in the enemy fortifications cut into the granite wall of the opposite gorge. No one expected to succeed, and the thirty men who volunteered to scramble over the chains in hope of destroying the machine-gun nests and redoubts considered themselves as good as dead. With grenades pinned to their chests and shoulders, and armed only with pistols, the thirty began to pull themselves, hand over hand, over the swaying chain bridge frame. Five hundred feet below, the river hissed white and seethed in a foamy boil.

The KMT machine guns squirted their orange bursts, and flying lead thudded into and battered the chain links and the acrobatic Reds. The soldiers kept coming, tossing grenades with one hand, while hanging to the frame with the other. Their comrades rained volleys of accurate shots into the astonished enemy nests.

Two Reds hurtled down into the river below,

one's arm shot away at the elbow, the other's face bashed into mush by the high-powered machine guns. But as the others drew closer to the opposite side they discovered that not all the boards had been removed. Not expecting an attack, the KMT garrison had left a quarter of the bridged planked. Now the Reds redoubled their efforts, hurling grenade after grenade into the nests. The KMT guards were shocked and incredulous: who were these monkeylike crawling devils so ready to die? They finally set out to destroy the remaining planks but the Red fire was too withering; all they could manage was to ignite the paraffin-soaked boards. Still the Reds advanced. One nest was smouldering, the machine gun twisted in a pathetic coil. One young Red as thin as a bamboo stalk and as agile as a cobra snaked himself over the remaining gun box and lobbed two grenades. More soldiers swung over the bridge; others were now on the planks. The KMT garrison fled screaming, their weapons glistening in the dewy morning grass.

Night. Mao is alone in his tent, his aides have gone to sleep hours before, Mao is not certain whether he is asleep or awake, the strain of the Tatu campaign has made everything seem strange. Mao hears the grinding rumble of a heavy tank and rushes from the tent. A tank, covered with peonies and laurel, advances toward him. Mao thinks the tank will crush him, but it presently clanks to a halt. The turret rises, hesitantly. Greta Garbo, dressed in red sealskin boots, red railway-man's cap and red satin coveralls, emerges. She speaks: "Mao, I have been bad in Moscow and wicked in Paris, I have been loved in every capital, but I have never met a MAN whom I could love. The man is you Mao, Mao, mine."

Mao considers this dialectically. The woman is clearly mad. Yet she is beautiful and the tank seems to work. How did she get through the sentries? Didn't the noise of the clanking tank treads wake the entire camp? Where is everyone?

Mao realizes the camp is empty. He is alone with Garbo. But Mao has always been more attracted to Harlow than to Garbo. What should he do not to break her romantic little heart?

"Madame, I have work to do,"says Mao gently.

"I can wait till tomorrow, my love," she answers, unzipping her coveralls.

Mao thinks: "After all, I have worked hard and do deserve a rest." But an internal voice answers him: "Rest only after socialism."

"My Mao, this is no way to treat a woman who has made a long journey to be with you."

"But what of my wife?"

"Ah, that is an old bourgeois ploy, Mao mine."

Garbo hangs her cap on the mouth of the tank's .375 recoilless cannon. And that night Mao instructed Garbo in the Chinese Way, the Five Paths, and the Three Encirclements.

"To regard all things and principles of things as inconstant modes or fashions has more and more become the tendency of modern thought. Let us begin with that which is without—our physical life. Fix upon it in one of its more exquisite intervals, the moment, for instance, of delicious recoil from the flood of water in summer heat. What is the whole physical life in that moment but a combination of natural elements

74   to which science gives their names? But these elements, phosphorus and lime and delicate fibres, are present not in the human body alone: we detect them in places most remote from it. Our physical life is a perpetual motion of them —the passage of the blood, the wasting and repairing of the lenses of the eye, the modification of the tissues of the brain by every ray of light and sound—processes which science reduces to simpler and more elementary forces. Like the elements of which we are composed, the action of these forces extends beyond us; it rusts iron and ripens corn. Far out on every side of us those elements are broadcast, driven by many forces; and birth and gesture and death and the springing violets from the grave are but a few out of ten thousand resultant combinations. That clear, perpetual outline of face and limb is but an image of ours, under which we group them—a design in a web, the actual threads of which pass out beyond it. This at least of flame-like our life has, that it is but the concurrence, renewed from moment to moment, of forces parting sooner or later on their ways.

"Or if we begin with the inward world of thought and feeling, the whirlpool is still more rapid, the flame more eager and devouring. There it is no longer the gradual darkening of the eye and fading of colour from the wall,—the movement of the shore-side, where the water flows down indeed, though in apparent rest,—but the race of the midstream, a drift of momentary acts of sight and passion and thought. At first sight experience seems to bury us under a flood of external objects, pressing upon us with a sharp and importunate reality, calling us out of ourselves in a thousand forms of action. But when

reflexion begins to act upon those objects they
are dissipated under its influence; the cohesive
force seems suspended like a trick of magic;
each object is loosed into a group of impressions
—colour, odour, texture—in the mind of the ob-
server. And if we continue to dwell in thought
on this world, not of objects in the solidity with
which language invests them, but of impressions
unstable, flickering, inconsistent, which burn
and are extinguished with our consciousness of
them, it contracts still further; the whole scope
of observation is dwarfed to the narrow chamber
of the individual mind. Experience, already reduced to a swarm of impressions, is ringed round
for each one of us by that thick wall of personality through which no real voice has ever pierced
on its way to us, or from us to that which we can
only conjecture to be without. Every one of those
impressions is the impression of the individual in
his isolation, each mind keeping as a solitary
prisoner its own dream of a world. Analysis goes
a step farther still, and assures us that those impressions of the individual mind to which, for
each one of us, experience dwindles down, are
in perpetual flight; that each of them is limited
by time, and that as time is infinitely divisible,
each of them is infinitely divisible also; all that
is actual in it being a single moment, gone while
we try to apprehend it, of which it may ever be
more truly said that it has ceased to be than that
it is. To such a tremulous wisp constantly re-
forming itself on the stream, to a single sharp
impression, with a sense in it, a relic more or less
fleeting, of such moments gone by, what is real
in our life fines itself down. It is with this movement, with the passage and dissolution of impressions, images, sensations, that analysis

leaves off—that continual vanishing away, that strange, perpetual weaving and unweaving of ourselves.

"*Philosophiren,* says Novalis, *ist dephlegma-tisiren vivificiren.* The service of philosophy, of speculative culture, towards the human spirit is to rouse, to startle it into sharp and eager observation. Every moment some form grows perfect in hand or face; some tone on the hills or the sea is choicer than the rest; some mood of passion or insight or intellectual excitement is irresistibly real and attractive for us—for that moment only. Not the fruit of experience, but experience itself, is the end. A counted number of pulses only is given to us of a variegated, dramatic life. How may we see in them all that is to be seen in them by the finest senses? How shall we pass most swiftly from point to point, and be present always at the focus where the greatest number of vital forces unite in their purest energy?

"To burn always with this hard, gemlike flame, to maintain this ecstasy, is success in life. In a sense it might even be said that our failure is to form habits: for, after all, habit is relative to a stereotyped world, and meantime it is only the roughness of the eye that makes any two persons, things, situations, seem alike. While all melts under our feet, we may well catch at any exquisite passion, or any contribution to knowledge that seems by a lifted horizon to set the spirit free for a moment, or any stirring of the senses, strange dyes, strange colours, and curious odours, or work of the artist's hands, or the face of one's friend. Not to discriminate every moment some passionate attitude in those about us, and in the brilliancy of their gifts some tragic dividing of forces on their ways, is, on this short day of frost and sun, to sleep before evening. With this sense of the splendour of our experience and of its awful brevity, gathering all we are into one desperate effort to see and touch, we shall hardly have time to make theories about the things we see and touch. What we have to do is to be forever curiously testing new opinions and courting new impressions, never acquiescing in a facile orthodoxy of Comte, or of Hegel, or of our own. Philosophical theories or ideas, as points of view, instruments of criticism, may help us to gather up what might otherwise pass unregarded by us. 'Philosophy is the microscope of thought.' The theory or idea or system which requires of us the sacrifice of any part of this experience, in consideration of some interest into which we cannot enter, or some abstract theory we have not identified with ourselves, or what is only conventional, has no real claim upon us.

"One of the most beautiful passages in the writings of Rousseau is that in the sixth book of the *Confessions,* where he describes the awakening in him of the literary sense. An undefinable taint of death had always clung about him, and now in early manhood he believed himself smitten by mortal disease. He asked himself how he might make as much as possible of the interval that remained; and he was not biased by anything in his previous life when he decided that it must be by intellectual excitement, which he found just then in the clear, fresh writings of Voltaire. Well! we are all *condamnés,* as Victor Hugo says: We are all under sentence of death but with a sort of indefinite reprieve—*les hommes sont tous condamnés à mort avec des sursis indéfinis:* We have an interval, and then our place knows us no more. Some spend this interval in listlessness, some in high passions, the wisest, at least among 'the children of this world,' in art and song. For our one chance lies in expanding that interval, in getting as many pulsations as possible into the given time. Great passions may give us this quickened sense of life, ecstasy and sorrow of love, the various forms of enthusiastic activity, disinterested or otherwise, which come naturally to many of us. Only be sure it is passion —that it does yield you this fruit of a quickened, multiplied consciousness. Of this wisdom, the poetic passion, the desire of beauty, the love of art for art's sake, has most; for art comes to you professing frankly to give you nothing but the highest quality to your moments as they pass, and simply for those moments' sake."

With the Tatu behind them the Red Army was comparatively safe but it was still confronted with the prospect of a two-thousand-mile march. Before them were seven huge mountain ranges, one desert, and a vast grassland, which could be reached only by first passing through a marsh-bog as large as the state of Georgia.

The man was brought before him. Mao was disconsolate. He had known the officer five years and had trusted him. Now it was discovered that this thin, bespectacled soldier had betrayed him, and Mao was chilled by the treachery.

"I can't believe this. Tell me yourself: are you the man?"

"Yes, Mao."

"But why?"

"We discovered him preparing another dispatch," one of the captors interrupted.

"Another dispatch! Is there no end to your double-dealing?"

"I did what I felt necessary and correct," the traitor answered staunchly. The snow fell heavily and heaps of powdery ice and snow clunked down from the overburdened pine boughs overhead. The little traitor's spectacles were running with snow and water, and Mao could not see his eyes.

"Were you paid to write these things — were you an agent for Chiang?"

"Yes, I was paid, poorly, for each of the articles, but I was and am in no one's service but the revolution's."

"He must be lying," shouted the culprit's discoverer.

"Let's shoot him now, Mao," said another officer. "Let's take him before the troops and show them how traitors are dealt with."

"No, leave me alone with him," Mao ordered. The officers left reluctantly, and one, with pistol drawn, hid himself behind a tree. Mao waved him off and he joined the others in their walk to the camp.

"Now tell me, Ling, what is all this about?"

"What's the fuss? I have been exercising my critical faculties on your poems and stories. Is that a great crime?"

"You have ridiculed my work in the reactionary press. You have been vicious in your explications and vengeful in your evaluations of my merit. I have harbored a serpent in my camp."

"All I have written is true, from my viewpoint. You are a mediocre talent, Mao. I respect you as my commander but scorn your pretensions to poetry."

"You hurt me, Ling. We have been through many campaigns together; your sister is my wife's third cousin; you were due for a promotion."

"Mao, your poetry does not improve as a consequence."

"Let's see what you were preparing to send off this time." The traitor produced a sheaf of papers and Mao tremblingly read a passage aloud: 'They have the pale tint of flowers that blossomed in too retired a shade—the coolness of meditative habit, which diffuses itself through feeling and observation of every sketch. Instead of passion there is sentiment: and, even in what purport to be pictures of actual life, we have allegory, not always so warmly dressed in its habiliments of flesh and blood as to be taken into the reader's mind without a shiver. Whether from lack of power, or an unconquerable reserve, the Author's touches have often an effect of tameness; the merriest man can hardly contrive to laugh at his broadest humor; the tenderest woman, one would suppose, will hardly shed warm tears at his deepest pathos. The book, if you would see anything in it, requires to be read in the clear, brown, twilight atmosphere in which it was written; if opened in the sunshine, it is apt to look exceedingly like a volume of blank pages.'

Mao ruminated over the passage and silently continued to read the remaining text.

"Apart from what you claim, Ling, your style is heavy and pompous."

"And your work is abstract and divorced from nature."

"Nature? Is that your model?"

'I look upon a great deal of the modern sentimentalism about Nature as a mark of disease. It is one more symptom of the general liver-complaint. To a man of wholesome constitution the wilderness is well enough for a mood or a vacation, but not for a habit of life. Those who have most loudly advertised their passion for seclusion and their intimacy with nature, from Petrarch down, have been mostly sentimentalists, unreal men, misanthropes on the spindle side, solacing an uneasy suspicion of themselves by professing contempt for their kind. They make demands on the world in advance proportioned to their inward measure of their own merit, and are angry that the world pays only by the visible measure of performance. It is true of Rousseau, the modern founder of the sect, true of Saint Pierre, his intellectual child, and of Châteaubriand, his grandchild, the inventor, we might almost say, of the primitive forest, and who first was touched by the solemn falling of a tree from natural decay in the windless silence of the woods. It is a very shallow view that affirms trees and rocks to be healthy, and cannot see that men in communities are just as true to the laws of their organization and destiny; that can tolerate the puffin and the fox, but not the fool and knave; that would shun politics because of its demagogues, and snuff up the stench of the obscene fungus. The divine life of Nature is more wonderful, more various, more sublime in man than in any other of her works, and the wisdom that is gained by commerce with men, as Montaigne and Shakespeare gained it, or with one's own soul among men, as Dante, is the most delightful, as it is the most precious of all. In outward nature it is still man that interests us, and we care far less for the things seen than the way in which they are seen by poetic eyes like Wordsworth's or Thoreau's, and the reflections they cast there. To hear the to-do that is often made over the simple fact that a man sees the image of himself in the outward world, one is reminded of a savage when he for the first time catches a glimpse of himself in a looking-glass.'

"Mao, whether art imitates nature or nature art, whether the worker of words finds the essential form through the hewn verbiage, or whether he creates the form as he goes along, whether you wear red underpants or white, or write in pencil or pen, whether you love ideas or men, will power and theory alone will not make you an artist."

"My dear Ling, I'm no longer angry with you. You are clearly a well-meaning fool. The work you have criticized is irrelevant to me. My major poem shall never be written—it is an idea in process, chaos formalized through evanescent action. My poem is in my head, and its documentation is a critical fiction left for others to write."

"That is all well and good for you, but what will you do with me?"

"Nothing, return to your men. Scribble as you please and keep your rifle clean."

"You're a good fellow, Mao."

"Keep your platitudes for your men, dear Ling. You will make a good cultural commissar after the revolution is won. Right now, leave me alone."

His spectacles frosted over, the critic stumbled toward camp. Mao removed a notebook from his pocket and wrote on a blank page: "Metaphor for a poem: how spectacles are like a lake in winter or how prisms are related to the revo-

lution—the gathering and refracting of envelop-
ing light." Mao thought for a moment and then
crossed the lines out. He wrote again: "Cherish
the ignorant and the half-sighted, they are the
revolution. The wise are the Great Harmony."

Across the Paotung Kang Mountain alone —
some 16,000 snow-capped feet above sea level
—the Communists lost two-thirds of their trans-
port animals, and hundreds of men were lost on
each mountain they climbed. By July, 1935, they
were able to pause in the flatlands and take stock
of their position. Nearly 90,000 men had left the
Kiangsi base nine months before, only 45,000
now remained. Some of the missing, however,
had stayed behind to fight a rear-guard action
against the pursuing KMT troops. Many remained
in the wake of Mao's trail as guerilla insur-
gents and revolutionary agitators; some settled
in villages and raised the families they had created in the course of their holding action.

One evening, before the troops were to resume
the trek, Mao, alone in his tent—his loyal aides
had left after a brief tea with their commander—
thought of what he had thus far accomplished.
Yes, he had fought destructive tendencies within
the party (Trotskyite elements had been extir-
pated), mustered the party to his support, suc-
cessfully resisted the Five Encirclements, and
strategically had withdrawn his troops for the
drive against the Japanese invasion in the north.
The Long March would indeed be recorded as a
major historical event. Mao could be proud, apart
from the glory of the Red Army's military suc-

cesses, of its achievements in liberating slaves, redistributing land and food among the poor, abolishing the warlords' taxes, enlisting the support of revolutionized young peasants—creating, in short, a new sensibility among all those the army had come into contact with.

Mao had accomplished much, but as he drowsed off to sleep on his hard pallet he thought the old rankling thought. He went over it once again. Stalin was married to a nobody, a pleasant soul but of no account politically or socially, and she was no beauty. But how many Russian women were? Ah, he could have used some of those Russian ladies on this trip, those tanks of women—*three* would have been enough for a regiment of his worn men. No. Stalin was no competition. Whatever the old fox did on the side didn't count, only real wives counted. Roosevelt's wife didn't count either, though he felt he would like to chat with her at tea. She would have been like a rich aunt.

Eva Braun stuck in his throat. She had disturbed his sleep even after the most exhausting day. Eva Braun was seductive. Not beautiful, certainly. But she drew you in like a great honey bog. She laughed; in all her photographs with Hitler she laughed. What did Hitler have? Perhaps nothing but his strut. How would Mao ever possess her or one like her? Was there an Eva for him?

Franco's wife was a dreary middle-class Spaniard, a rosary-kissing midget, as sexy as a decayed turnip. And what was Franco but a pint-sized Madonna-lover and Pope-kisser? And Spain itself: a land of mustachioed ladies with oily skin. In the most recent issue of *National Geographic* Mao had seen many pictures of

Spanish ladies in their silly costumes, none of
whom Mao would have given a chopstick for.

Il Duce was another wound, perhaps one more
festering than Hitler. What eyes his woman had!
Little electric shivers of green passed between
her lashes. What style, what authentic woman-
hood. How did she walk? With short, shuffling
steps, like the Peiping beauties; with the gangling
gait and cowboy strut of the American girls, or
perhaps with that exquisite long slither and half
prance—part snake, part doe—of the French and
Italians? Claretta, what was the marvellous creature but the Mediterranean itself, stormy and
calm and ageless. But was she the stout man's
real wife? Mussolini behaved in public as if she
were. He took her to the opera. What did it mean?
Those Italians were strange.

Mao regarded his own condition: One wife
dead. Another pregnant. Attractive. A good comrade. Loyal. But was that enough for a poet, for
a man who loved delicate things, such as the
frozen crystal-candied branches of birch trees in
a moony winter night, and intellectual conversation with a sophisticated, beautiful female
companion?

What could he do? Could he leave his second
wife?...What would his comrades think and say?
But what was more important: to live by the lights
of duty (and suffer) or to assume the responsibil-
ity for one's own true desires and be sometimes
happy, though unrespectable? He was forty-five
years old; he could not wait much longer to start
a new life. With the revolution over, he could retire, and with a wife like Claretta he could write
poetry till all the sampans in China went down to
the sea. He would have to think of this matter
more. There were many miles left of the long

journey, and Claretta and Eva would doubtlessly haunt him again.

No sooner had the Red Army crossed the mountains than it sank in the boglands of the Mantzu territory. The tribesmen of the region were unapproachable. Like the hostile Lolos, they too hated the Chinese but, unlike them, they permitted no negotiation or discussion. They simply took the Reds as their enemies, as they would any Chinese, and set out to fight them. For the first time the Reds were faced with a guerrilla war directed against *them.* The Mantzu burned their own houses, hid food and livestock, leveled bare everything in the Red Army's path. The Communists could neither buy nor barter for food; the sorties they made in the interior usually cost the lives of two soldiers for every cow or sheep or chicken or dove or egg they took. And even if there had been food, there was no fire to cook it.

"I had just finished breakfast, and was lying on my back smoking. A bullet whistled so unusually low as to attract my attention and struck with a loud smash in a tree about twenty feet from me. Between me and the tree a soldier with his greatcoat rolled under his head for a pillow lay on his back reading a newspaper which he held in both hands. I remember smiling to myself to see this man start as the bullet passed. Some of his comrades left off playing cards and looked for it. The man who was reading remained perfectly still, his eyes fixed on the paper with a steadiness which I thought curious, considering the bustle around him. Presently I noticed that there were a few drops of blood on his neck, and that his face was paling. Calling to the card players, who had resumed their game, I said, 'See to that man with the paper.' They went to him, spoke to him, touched him, and found him perfectly dead. The ball had struck him under the chin, traversed the neck, and cut the spinal column where it joins the brain, making a fearful hole through which the blood had already soaked his greatcoat. It was this man's head and not the tree which had been struck with such a report. There he lay, still holding the New York *Independent,* with his eyes fixed on a sermon by Henry Ward Beecher. It was really quite a remarkable circumstance."

The swampland provided no fuel, and had there been any, it would not have mattered, since it rained for fourteen days and nights. Nothing could be ignited in that downpour. No food and no fire and no shelter. The men huddled together in the night rain, their clothes soaked, their stomachs loose and sour. Chilled, shivering, hungry, and tired. Nothing but rainy sky and wet green marsh. No tree to shit behind. No warm cave to rest in during the rainy, chilly nights. No food but green wheat and raw turnips and, occasionally, a raw, flayed rabbit. Clothes stinking and rotting on the flesh. The flesh sagging, the eyes popping, and balls banging in their flappy sacs.
"Is this a revolution?" Mao asked himself as he sat on his hams to write a poem about The Long March. "Revolution? This is the shits, kiddo," he whispered to the wet grass.

("Surely, the aim of a true philosophy must lie, not in futile efforts towards the complete accommodation of man to the circumstances in which he chances to find himself, but in the maintenance of a kind of candid discontent, in the face of the very highest achievement; the unclouded and receptive soul quitting the world finally, with the same fresh wonder with which it had entered the world still unimpaired, and going on its blind way at last with the consciousness of some profound enigma in things, as but a pledge of something further to come. Marius seemed to understand how one might look back upon life here, and its excellent visions, as but the portion of a race-course left behind him by a runner still swift of foot: for a moment he experienced a singular curiosity, almost an ardent desire to enter upon a future, the possibilities of which seemed so large.")

"Remember therefore always, you have two characters in which all greatness of art consists: First, the earnest and intense seizing of natural facts; then the ordering of those facts by strength of human intellect, so as to make them for all who look upon them, to the utmost serviceable, memorable, and beautiful. And thus great art is nothing else than the type of strong and noble life; for as the ignoble person, in his dealings with all that occurs in the world about him, first sees nothing clearly—looks nothing fairly in the face, and then allows himself to be swept away by the trampling torrent, and unescapable force, of the things that he would not foresee and could not understand: so the noble person, looking the facts of the world full in the face, and fathoming them with deep faculty, then deals with them in unalarmed intelligence and unhurried strength, and becomes, with his human intellect and will, no unconscious nor insignificant agent in consummating their good and restraining their evil.

"Thus in human life you have two fields of rightful toil for ever distinguished, yet for ever associated: Truth first—plan or design, founded thereon: so in art, you have the same two fields for ever distinguished, for ever associated; Truth first—plan, or design, founded thereon.

"Now hitherto there is not the least difficulty in the subject; none of you can look for a moment at any great sculptor or painter without seeing the full bearing of these principles."

Three men carried a mangled corpse on a wooden door. Mao looked up from his tea.

"Who is he?"

"One of the villagers who helped us. He was tortured."

"Did he talk?" Mao asked.

"We have reason to believe so. Others who had helped us were also shot."

"What did they do to him?"

"Tore out his teeth and seared his gums with hot coals. Some say he refused to speak even then, but he spoke when they broke his son's fingers with a stone."

"They burned his hut, too, and starved out his wife and children."

"Where are they?"

"With friends, but there is hardly enough food to share."

"How did they choose him among the villagers?"

"Some think there was an informer."

"In one of the late movements of our troops in the valley (near Upperville, I think), a strong force of Moseby's mounted guerillas attacked a train of wounded and the guard of cavalry convoying them. The ambulances contained about 60 wounded, quite a number of them officers of rank. The rebels were in strength, and the capture of the train and its partial guard after a short snap was effectually accomplished. No sooner had our men surrendered, the rebels instantly commenced robbing the train and murdering their prisoners, even the wounded. Here is the scene or a sample of it, ten minutes after. Among the wounded officers in the ambulances were one, a lieutenant of regulars, and another of higher rank. These two were dragged out on the ground on their backs, and were now surrounded by the guerillas, a demoniac crowd, each member of which was stabbing them in different parts of their bodies. One of the officers had his feet pinned firmly to the ground by bayonets stuck through them and thrust into the ground. These two officers, as afterward found on examination, had received about twenty such thrusts, some of them through the mouth, face, etc. The wounded had all been dragged (to give a better chance also for plunder) out of their wagons; some had been effectually dispatched, and their bodies were lying there lifeless and bloody. Others not yet dead, but horribly mutilated, were moaning or groaning. Of our men who surrendered, most had been thus maimed or slaughtered.

"At this instant a force of our cavalry, who had been following the train at some interval, charged suddenly upon the secesh captors, who proceeded at once to make the best escape they could. Most of them got away, but we gobbled two officers and seventeen men, in the very acts just described. The sight was one which admitted of little discussion, as may be imagined. The seventeen captured men and two officers were put under guard for the night, but it was decided there and then that they should die. The next morning the two officers were taken in the town, separate places, put in the center of the street, and shot. The seventeen men were taken to an open ground, a little one side. They were placed in a hollow square, half-encompassed by two of our cavalry regiments, one of which regiments had three days before found the bloody corpses of three of their men hamstrung and hung up by the heels to limbs of trees by Moseby's guerillas, and the other had not long before had twelve men, after surrendering, shot and then hung by the neck to limbs of trees, and jeering inscriptions pinned to the breast of one of the corpses, who had been a sergeant. Those three, and those twelve, had been found, I say, by these environing regiments. Now, with revolvers, they formed the grim cordon of the seventeen prisoners. The latter were placed in the midst of the hollow square, unfastened, and the ironical remark made to them that they were now to be given 'a chance for themselves.' A few ran for it. But what use? From every side the deadly pills came. In a few minutes the seventeen corpses strewed the hollow square. I was curious to know whether some of the Union soldiers, some few (some one or two at least of the youngsters), did not abstain from shooting on the helpless men. Not one. There was no exultation, very little said, almost nothing, yet every man there contributed his shot.

"Multiply the above by scores, aye hundreds —verify it in all the forms that different circumstances, individuals, places, could afford—light it with every lurid passion, the wolf's, the lion's lapping thirst for blood—the passionate, boiling volcanoes of human revenge for comrades, brothers slain—with the light of burning farms, and heaps of smutting, smoldering black embers — and in the human heart everywhere black, worse embers—and you have an inkling of this war."

A great wave of nausea spread over Mao, a heaviness of revulsion and defeat. How could one win? They owned everything. They had the guns and the troops and the presses and the streets. They held the universities and the theatres and the ships; they manufactured nails and doorknobs, paper, steel, radios, toothpicks, eyeglasses and chairs. They could bribe and buy their adversaries, or frighten them or force them from their jobs, invade their homes, arrest, beat, kill them secretly or murder them publicly. How was one to endure? No sooner did five men band together than they were dragged to prison. Whom could you trust? Neighbors, colleagues, relatives—all were to be suspect of informing to the enemy, and each man felt himself alone. Each man felt himself a stranger in his family and country, felt alone with his dissent and rebellion. Alone under a vast leaden-lidded sky.

Mao left camp and wandered across a flat stony field until he came to a wide muddy river. The bank opposite grew luxuriant with Brazil trees and leafy oaks, drooping branches of weeping willows trailed in the still water. Nothing stirred, but suddenly the wet air smelled of nitrate and chrysanthemums.

Mao was about to return to camp when, seemingly from nowhere, a sampan glided toward him. Its bow was festooned with lilies and forget-me-nots, bluebells and red tulips; black and purple velvet shrouded the stern. The craft left no wake as it soundlessly cleaved the water. A cowled figure stood midship and propelled the boat with long rhythmical strokes of a single silver oar.

"Why do you dawdle there?" the man asked, as the boat prowed into the mucky bank.

"What is on the other side?" Mao asked in return.

"Nothing."

"Ferry me there."

"First remove your boots and uniform."

Mao reluctantly obeyed, leaving his canteen, Colt 45, muddy boots, denim pants, and quilted coat in a tidy pile beside him. Naked, Mao's ribs showed through his skinny chest. Little sheets of ice formed at the river edge, and the ground where Mao sat was frozen hard, and although minutes before when fully clothed he had shivered, Mao did not feel cold now.

"Before you come aboard, I must shave your head and pare your nails."

Mao allowed this to be done.

"Shall we ever arrive at the opposite shore?" Mao asked, seating himself in a niche between the flowers and the velvet.

"It's not a question of arriving, Mao, but of returning."

"Is that not the same process?"

"For some."

Fatigued, Mao stretched himself out and closed his eyes. When he woke he was sitting cross-legged on a grassy bank. The sampan was gone, and with it his clothes and pistol. A nightingale sang in a bough above Mao's head, then fluttered away when Mao raised his eyes toward it. A chubby jade-green snake slithered by and forked his pink tongue at Mao's toes.

"Watch your feet," the snake said.

"A talking snake? A most supranatural snake!"

"A snake who would live, sir."

"Judging by your girth, you seem to live well enough."

"That is my aim."

"Do the other serpents here speak too?"

"I don't know, I haven't seen others."

"Alone, eh? Like me. Are you a wise snake?"

"As wise as need be."

"Do you have any wisdom or temptations for me?"

"None more than you already possess, but I can improvise."

"Proceed."

"Keep your thoughts and sell your clothes."

"That's a strange aphorism to come from one so well fed as you."

"Quite right. How about, Three squares a day keeps famine away."

"You are trite for a talking snake."

"Loneliness does dull one."

"Why lonely?"

"I am unique, alone with my vision."

"I understand you, snake."

"Well, I'm off now, Mao. There is a fat brown mouse to attend to, and, besides, there's a hawk circling about who seems interested in me."

"Hurry and farewell, dear snake. I regret this has been so pointless an interview."

"Farewell, Mao. Don't fall into despair," the snake advised as he slid among toadstools and crashed into the shrubbery.

"Despair? There is enough now in me to fill three worlds. Why is the world this way? This dirty road. This rending, loveless path. You *are* alone, Mao. All friendships transitory, all accomplishments irrelevant. Everything, including the revolution, mere spider threads of hopes and illusion. Does the revolution you so much love love you? Does it nurse your tired feet? Does it warm and caress your stinking, worn body after a day's march? Will it spark life into your dead dust. How does it figure?"

Years before similar questions had troubled Mao: Who was he to assume such special knowledge; how could he dare sunder himself from the common fate—what did life hold in store for him? In thinking these thoughts he only further removed himself from those with whom he so dearly wished to connect. He shied away from friends and family. He roamed the outskirts of his village, watching the clouds glide over clear minnow pools, and "On the few occasions when he came out from his immediate haunts into the village, he had a strange owllike appearance, uncombed, unbrushed, his hair long and tangled; his face, they said, darkened with smoke, his cheeks pale, the indentation of his brow deeper than ever before; an earnest, haggard, sulking look; and so he went hastily along the village street, feeling as if all eyes might find out what he had in his mind from his appearance; taking by-ways where they were to be found, going long distances through woods and fields, rather than short ones where the way lay through the frequented haunts of men.

"For he shunned the glances of his fellow-men, probably, because he had learned to consider them not as fellows, because he was seeking to withdraw himself from the common bond and destiny,—because he felt, too, that on that account his fellow-men would consider him as a traitor, an enemy, one who had deserted their cause, and tried to withdraw his feeble shoulder from under that great burden of death which is imposed on all men to bear, and which, if one could escape, each other would feel his load proportionately heavier. With these beings of a moment he had no longer any common cause; they must go their separate ways, yet apparently the same,—they on the broad, dusty beaten path, that always seemed full, but from which continually they seemed so strangely vanished into invisibility, no one knowing, or long inquiring, what had become of them; he on his lonely path, where he should tread secure, with no trouble but the loneliness, which would be none to him."

The water ruffled. It spoke to him. "Mao, enough of this. Join me. Bath in me. Submerge yourself."

Mao considered the invitation, wondering if with one long last diving swim deep to the bottom, down to the oozy bed and tangled weeds, far down, below where the minnows darted and the waterbugs skimmed, wondering if, finally, he could dissolve himself in the watery merge.

"Mao, dissolve in me, float with the silt and algae. Suspend yourself in the living solution."

"Some solution! Should I cash in this willful flesh for a sack of fishmeal?"

"Mao," the spirit of the water murmured, 'to cease from action—the ending of thine own effort to think and do: there is no evil in that. Turn thy thought to the ages of man's life, boyhood, youth, maturity, old age: the change in every one of these also is a dying, but evil nowhere. Thou climbedst into the ship, thou hast made thy voyage and touched the shore: go forth now! Be it into some other life: the divine breath is everywhere, even there. Be it into forgetfulness for ever; at least thou wilt rest from the beating of sensible images upon thee, from the passions which pluck thee this way and that like an unfeeling toy, from those long marches of the intellect, from thy toilsome ministry to the flesh.'

"True, and I've had enough of that. Here we

come then." Mao waded into the river until only
his head showed above the flat surface. He remained that way for several minutes, neither
warm nor cold, neither awake nor asleep, neither
happy nor sad.

"What's the use," Mao said, as he began a slow
frog-stroke far out to the river.

"He ceased swimming, but the moment he felt
the water rising above his mouth the hands
struck out sharply with a lifting movement. The
will to live, was his thought, and the thought was
accompanied by a sneer. Well, he had will,—ay,
will strong enough that with one last exertion it
could destroy itself and cease to be.

"He changed his position to a vertical one. He
glanced up at the quiet stars, at the same time
emptying his lungs of air. With swift, vigorous
propulsion of hands and feet, he lifted his shoulders and half his chest out of the water. This was
to gain impetus for the descent. Then he let himself go and sank without movement, a white
statue, into the sea. He breathed in the water
deeply, deliberately, after the manner of a man
taking an anaesthetic. When he strangled, quite
involuntarily his arms and legs clawed the water
and drove him up to the surface and into the clear
sights of the stars.

"The will to live, he thought disdainfully, vainly
endeavoring not to breathe the air into his bursting lungs. Well, he would have to try a new way.
He filled his lungs with air, filled them full. This
supply would take him far down. He turned over
and went down head first, swimming with all his
strength and all his will. Deeper and deeper he
went. His eyes were open, and he watched the
ghostly, phosphorescent trails of the darting bo-
nita. As he swam, he hoped that they would not
strike at him, for it might snap the tension of his

will. But they did not strike, and he found time to be grateful for this last kindness of life.

"Down, down, he swam till his arms and legs grew tired and hardly moved. He knew that he was deep. The pressure on his ear-drums was a pain, and there was a buzzing in his head. His endurance was faltering, but he compelled his arms and legs to drive him deeper until his will snapped and the air drove from his lungs in a great explosive rush. The bubbles rubbed and bounded like tiny balloons against his cheeks and eyes as they took their upward flight. Then came pain and strangulation. This hurt was not death, was the thought that oscillated through his reeling consciousness. Death did not hurt. It was life, the pangs of life, this awful, suffocating feeling; it was the last blow life could deal him.

"His willful hands and feet began to beat and churn about, spasmodically and feebly. But he had fooled them and the will to live that made them beat and churn. He was too deep down. They could never bring him to the surface. He seemed floating languidly in a sea of dreamy vision. Colors and radiances surrounded him and bathed him and pervaded him. What was that? It seemed a lighthouse; but it was inside his brain—a flashing, bright white light." It cautioned him that he soon would crack into the deepest night rocks, where there were no more long marches, only an endless, soggy, advancing and retreating flow, a timeless wafting and insentient drifting, a dumbness to the coursing world. The new Mao: a hectic mist upon the lakes and mountains, trillions of divorced atoms charging among cities, fields and oceans. To be everything and nothing, a *lumpen organismus*. What was the logic of that? What did his body ever do for him that he should be its conscience and destroyer? Wasn't his body after all, exploiting the capital formation of his thoughts, thriving on the surplus value of his mind and gorging itself on his will? Should he now play proletariat to the Universal arch-capitalist, should he kowtow to his stupid flesh? Should he be the raw stuffs to a voracious cosmos?

Up he shot, until he broke into the airy day. And by no reason of his own effort, Mao found himself back on the bank from which he had taken the sampan. Shivering, he returned to his bewildered camp just as the frosted moon and icicled stars surfaced above the steaming black kettles and redorange watchfires.

During the last two days of the journey through the Mantzu swamps and grasslands, Mao was sick with dysentery and chills. He had to be transported on a stretcher made of a U.S.A. World War I army blanket, moth-eaten and frayed. Mao's elbow had ripped the Kleenex-thin material, and there was no time to stop and mend the tear. The Reds jogged along an old trail, daring not even to pause and return the fire the Mantzus had been raining on them from behind the cover of the grass and reeds that grew thick and taller than a man, right up to the trail's edge. The Reds who fell on that trailway were given shallow burials: a handful of earth and reeds thrown over the eyes and face.

Mao grew worse. He spoke in his sleep and shivered under piles of soggy blankets. His wife frequently brought him bowls of cold rice and rabbit meat, but Mao was unable to keep his teeth from chattering long enough to eat anything. Everyone waited for Mao to give up his yellow ghost. Mao felt his spirit about to fly out of his mouth when a great cry went up from his scouts. They had come to the end of the grasslands. The Reds were now in hospitable country, only two weeks away from the soviet base at Shensi. On October 20, 1935, one year after they had fled Kiangsi, the 20,000 survivors of The Long March arrived at the Red sanctuary.

"The advance of the season now became as rapid as its first approach had been tedious and lingering. The days were uniformly mild, while the nights, though cool, were no longer chilled by frosts. The whippoorwill was heard whistling his melancholy notes along the margin of the lake, and the ponds and meadows were sending forth the music of their thousand tenants. The leaf of the native poplar was seen quivering in the woods; the sides of the mountains began to lose their hue of brown, as the lively green of the different members of the forest blended their shades with the permanent colors of the pine and hemlock; and even the buds of the tardy oak were swelling with the promise of the coming summer. The gay and fluttering bluebird, the social robin, and the industrious little wren were all to be seen enlivening the fields with their presence and their songs; while the soaring fish hawk was already hovering over the waters of the Otsego, watching, with native voracity, for the appearance of his prey."

The field was covered with men stretched out in the warming sun. The soldiers smoked cigarettes and drank tea and dreamed of roast ducks stuffed with chestnuts. Mao sat apart from his men, under a young weeping willow tree. He wanted to write a sonnet celebrating the victory

of The Long March, but images confusedly
streamed in his mind. He was distracted.

In the open field before him, a hundred flowers
bloomed side by side, each bathed in the sun,
each held in the wind's sway, each deeply rooted
in the rich, dark soil. Flowers, acre after acre,
flowers far down to the horizon line, where they
glowed yellow and red, tinting the margin of the
pale, algid sky above them. Through his binoculars Mao could see poppies, sunflowers,
daffodils, dogwoods, tigerflowers, Queen-
Anne's-Lace, lilacs, bunchberries, rhododen-
drons, blazing stars, lahuas, jasmines, violets,
carnations, cornflowers, milkweeds, mountain
laurels, bedstraws, syringas, forget-me-nots,
yarrows, magnolias, red clovers, galias, golden-
rods, columbines, chicory, black-eyed-susans,
peach blossoms, cromwells, zinnias, blue-
bonnets, lilies, lupines, roses, buttercups, sham-
rocks, sticktights, spiderworts, morning glories,
hankweeds, china pinks, peonies, orchids, geraniums, gardenias, asters, bloodroots, bugs-
banes, chamomiles, wintergreens, hyacinths,
irises, gentians, morning flowers, tulips, cream-
cups, cinquefoils, morning glories, groundsels,
adder's tongues, bluets, self-heals, pasque-
flowers, bouncing belts, vervains, spring beauties, thistles, fireweeds, redmaids, godetias,
beebalms, groomwells, saxifrages, safflowers;
Mao recognized, interspersed among these,
clusters of no less attractive but harmful and
poisonous plants and flowers breathing in the
same air as the others, bathing in the same sun,
fastened in the same soil: May apples, upases,
polkweeds, black nightshades, jimson weeds,
water hemlocks, poison ivies, poison sumacs,
foxgloves, henbanes, sheep laurels, monks-
hoods, castor-oil plants, death camasses, bella-

donnas, poison berries, poison laurels, poison rhubarbs, mayweeds, poison bays, poison bulbs, red buckeyes, poison rye grasses, poison peas, poison weeds.

Mao put down his binoculars. He sighed. The poem would not come. He would wait for a better time. Something was making him apprehensive. He studied the field again—all those growths living in seeming harmony, the ill with the good. This is what occurs when nature flourishes naturally, but a good gardener uproots the killing weeds and prunes the decaying branches from the living trees. Must one do to nations what is required of gardens? Still, may one transpose metaphors from nature to art without risking the purity of the image?

Mao's wife brought him a pot of tea. She seemed happy.

"We have won, my dear husband."

"Perhaps," Mao answered, averting his eyes. There was no finer day than this, but Mao was disturbed by an unpleasant and frightening thought, his Poem was over.

The interview with Chairman Mao was granted on the condition it would not be published in any mass-audience periodical and that no photographs be printed. The interview was conducted with the aid of an interpreter, although Chairman Mao did speak an occasional sentence in French and English: he reads both languages. Part of the interview, concerning such matters as the personal life of the interviewers and social and political issues, has been omitted as not having direct relation to the substance of the interview. For example, Chairman Mao asked the interviewer if he had children and if so, how many, were they all by the same woman, their ages, et cetera. Mao also asked questions that had economic and social interest to him: the interviewer's annual salary, the monthly cost of food and shelter for a skilled worker, and so on. In short, Mao conducted his own interview before we entered the discussion here transcribed. The conversation took place in Chairman Mao's house in the spring of 1968.

Chairman Mao's study merits description. The room is severely furnished: four cane-bottomed chairs: a round pine table by a window, the sill of which is cluttered with pots of geraniums and what seem to be a hundred varieties of flowers flourishing in confusion. The table is heaped with brand-new and old books, magazines, periodicals, and catalogues from museums and gallery exhibitions. Among the more familiar are: *Art and Artist, Arts Magazine, Art Forum, Art News, Art International, Studio, Encounter, Esquire, Metro, Partisan Review, The Nation, National Review, Monthly Review, New York Review of Books, Dissent, Vogue, Poetry, Evergreen Review, Chelsea Review, Film Quarterly, Sight* and Sound, *Films in Review, Cinema, Film Heritage, Movie, New York Film Bulletin, Cahiers du Cinéma, Tri-Quarterly, Journal of Aesthetics, Journal of Popular Culture, PMLA, American Literature, American Literature Quarterly, Critique, Wisconsin Studies in Criticism, Harper's Bazaar, Playboy, Science and Society, Daedalus, Thoreau Society Bulletin, New Left Review, National Geographic, Atlas.* Books: *Love's Body, Understanding Media, Against Interpretation, Second Skin, Come Back, Dr. Caligari, Armies of the Night, Why Are We in Vietnam?, In Cold Blood, The Confessions of Nat Turner, The Poems of Wallace Stevens, Concrete Poetry, Ariel, For the Union Dead, Howl, The Poems of E. A. Poe, Collected Poems of W. H. Auden, The Adventures of Sinbad the Sailor, Twenty Thousand Leagues Under the Sea, The Count of Monte Cristo, The Adventures of Robin Hood, The Three Musketeers, Moby Dick, Tin Tin: Journey to the Moon, The Iron Heel, A Farewell to Arms.*

On the walls, pinned, pasted, or hung were reproductions of paintings and posters for art shows in the United States and photographs and stills of personalities and films, and of Chinese heroes and Mao's comrades on The Long March. A picture from *Paris Match* of the Red Guards marching was placed between reproductions of a Cézanne portrait of Mme Cézanne and an Ingres *Le Bain;* Lenin in railroad worker's cap edged beside Godard looking up at a film strip; an announcement for a Trova exhibition—a potbellied chrome man on the verge of falling—was pasted below a still of Bardot and Moreau in *Viva Maria,* the two women reclined expectantly by a Gatling gun. This still was pressed beside a "See the Alps in Spring" color poster of golden-rods on an alpine hillside; a picture of Castro smiling into torn space—the other half of the photograph, with Krushchev embracing the Cuban leader at the United Nations, was nowhere on the wall. Hanging alone was a large poster of Che in a maroon beret, his eyes turned up to heaven.

Interviewer: Are you preparing an edition of your poems for publication in the near future?

Mao: This is a tactful way of asking me if I have written any new poems, isn't it?

I: In part, yes.

Mao: Well, some years ago I received an invitation from the YMHA in New York to give a reading. At first I thought I would like to read new poems, poems that have broken away from the Han dynasty influence, poems I could consider truly revolutionary, which would be worthy of the honor of such an invitation. But I hadn't as yet written those poems, so I thought I would wait a bit until I had. Now I think I will never give that reading. Naturally, there are other considerations for this postponement.

I: Would you care to explain that?

Mao: I didn't intend to be vague. It is simply that I have become preoccupied with other things. Aesthetics, the philosophy of art, and contemporary American art have taken hold of my imagination for some while, and so too, recently, the Red Guards as an aesthetic myth, for example ... but perhaps we shall discuss that later.

I: By philosophy of art and aesthetics you mean Marxist philosophy, Marxist aesthetics?

Mao: I suppose the reply should be Marxist/

Leninist or Mao/Marxist aesthetics—something like that. Naturally I do mean that, too. Simply, I have been thinking and studying about what art means to me.

I: Isn't that kind of individual reaction to art antithetic to the concerns and good of the state?

Mao: As I conceive it, all our progress is to exploit the state so that it makes such speculation possible.

I: Well, in what way than *do* you see the function of the state?

Mao: "The State is to be a voluntary manufacturer and distributor of necessary commodities. The State is to make what is useful. The individual is to make what is beautiful. And as I have mentioned the word labour, I cannot help saying that a great deal of nonsense is being written and talked nowadays about the dignity of manual labour. There is nothing necessarily dignified about manual labour at all, and most of it is absolutely degrading. It is mentally and morally injurious to man to do anything in which he does not find pleasure, and many forms of labour are quite pleasureless activities, and should be regarded as such. To sweep a slushy crossing for eight hours on a day when the east wind is blowing is a disgusting occupation. To sweep it with mental, moral, or physical dignity seems to me to be impossible. To sweep it with joy would be appalling. Man is made for something better than disturbing dirt. All work of that kind should be done by a machine.

"And I have no doubt that it will be so. Up to the present, man has been, to a certain extent, the slave of machinery, and there is something tragic in the fact that as soon as man had invented a machine to do his work he began to starve. This, however, is, of course, the result of our property and our system of competition. One man owns a machine which does the work of five hundred men. Five hundred men are, in consequence, thrown out of employment, and, having no work to do, become hungry and take to thieving. The one man secures the produce of the machine and keeps it, and has five hundred times as much as he should have, and probably, which is of much more importance, a great deal more than he really wants. Were that machine the property of all, everybody would benefit by it. It would be an immense advantage to the community. All unintellectual labour, all monotonous, dull labour, all labour that deals with dreadful things, and involves unpleasant conditions, must be done by machinery. Machinery must work for us in coal mines, and do all sanitary services, and be the stoker of streamers, and clean the streets, and run messages on wet days, and do anything that is tedious or distressing. At present machinery competes against man. Under proper conditions machinery will serve man. There is no doubt at all that this is the future of machinery; and just as trees grow while the country gentleman is asleep, so while Humanity will be amusing itself, or enjoying cultivated leisure—which, and not labour, is the aim of man—or making beautiful things, or reading beautiful things, or simply contemplating the world with admiration and delight, machinery will be doing all the necessary and unpleasant work. The fact is, that civilization requires slaves. The Greeks were quite right there. Unless there are slaves to do the ugly, horrible, uninteresting work, culture and contemplation become almost impossible. Human slavery is wrong, insecure, and demoralizing. On mechanical slavery, on the slavery of the machine, the future of the world depends. And when scientific men are no longer called upon to go down to a depressing East End and distribute bad cocoa and worse blankets to starving people, they will have delightful leisure in which to devise wonderful and marvellous things for their own joy and the joy of every one else. There will be great storages of force for every city, and for every house if required, and this force man will convert into light, or motion, according to his needs. Is this Utopian? A map of the world that does not include Utopia is not worth even glancing at, for it leaves out the one country at which Humanity is always landing. And when Humanity lands there, it looks out, and, seeing a better country, sets sail. Progress is the realization of Utopias.

"Now, I have said that the community by means of organization of machinery will supply the useful things, and that the beautiful things will be made by the individual. This is not merely necessary, but it is the only possible way by which we can get either the one or the other. An individual who has to make things for the use of others, and with reference to their wants and their wishes, does not work with interest, and consequently cannot put into his work what is best in him. Upon the other hand, whenever a community or a powerful section of a community, or a government of any kind, attempts to dictate to the artist what he is to do, Art either entirely vanishes, or becomes stereotyped, or degenerates into a low and ignoble form of craft. A work of art is the unique result of a unique temperament. Its beauty comes from the fact that the author is what he is. It has nothing to do with the fact that other people want what they want. Indeed, the moment that an artist takes notice of what other people want, and tries to supply the demand, he ceases to be an artist, and becomes a dull or an amusing craftsman, an honest or a dishonest tradesman. He has no further claim to be considered as an artist. Art is the most intense mood of Individualism that the world has known. I am inclined to say that it is the only real mode of Individualism that the world has known."

I: It seems to me that what you say now bears little resemblance to your position in the famous Yenan conference of 1942.

Mao: Yes, I did say in 1942 that there are two criteria for discussing art: aesthetic and political. (Mao rose and, taking a worn volume from a bookcase made of Florida orange-crates, began reading): "We know there is a political standard and an artistic standard. What is the proper relation between them? Politics is not at the same time art. The world outlook in general is not at the same time the methods of artistic creation. Not only do we reject abstract and rigid political standards but we also reject abstract and rigid artistic standards. Different class societies have different political and artistic standards as do the various classes within a given class society. But in any class society or in any class within that society, political standards come first and artistic standards come second."

I: Is that an oblique way of saying what Trotsky professed in *Literature and Revolution,* that we must not confuse art *for* the revolution with revolutionary art; or with art that arises after the establishment of socialism?

Mao: Yes, if by "after the establishment of socialism" you mean a time of Great Harmony, in which *class* struggles have been eliminated and transcendental explorations will have begun, then I agree. And it is for that reason that the most revolutionary art may bring—in the terms in which we were speaking—the most unwanted consequences, at least at *this* moment in our culture. The work of Morris, Judd, and Smithson, Andre, and Tony Smith, for example, are stupendously Eastern (Old East) and revolutionary but of questionable value in our immediate struggle.

I: Pardon me, but it seems, so far in our conversation, that you are more interested in revolutionary art than in art for the revolution. Or what else explains your involvement with contemporary bourgeois art?

Mao: Let's say that my wife and I have established a dialectical relationship in this regard. She is responsible for the cultural

present—the opera and stage and so on—
and I am responsible for preparing the
theoretical groundwork for the future ...
for the time of the Great Harmony. My wife
is ideologically closer to where I was in the
1930's and 1940's than I am now. I do not
renounce my former position; I merely
wish to work on two levels or planes, and
what I think is pertinent now is not necessarily what I think will be of future value
or pertinence. You might say that my wife's
spirit is with the Old Left, mine with the
New. (Here Mao and the interpreter
laughed.) My wife has always been more
fond than I of slogans and banners. (More
laughter.)

I: Do you feel there is social relevance in
your attitudes and goals?

Mao: In fact, I am not interested in that. If it were
possible, I would have long ago aban-
doned the world—most men are moral
monsters and fools and not worth a glance,
let alone a conversation. Had I not my work
to sustain me daily, I would poison myself
on bitterness.

I: What brought on this sudden acrimony?

Mao: Self-indulgence and long memory.

I: Memory of what?

Mao: Of the world and its human inhabitants.

I: With human nature?

Mao: With natural humans.

I: Can they be changed?

Mao: Lenin kept saucers of milk in his rooms so
that his cats could drink wherever they
found themselves. He loved cats.

I: Are you implying that Lenin did not love
men?

Mao: No one can who has lived with them.

I: And cats?

Mao: Any animal is preferable to a human, in the long run.

I: Does your attitude speak for a self-hate?

Mao: Your suggestion is facile and inaccurate. Are you so inexperienced, do you so much lack a knowledge of history, not to understand what I am saying?

I: Surely, Chairman Mao, your disregard for men is nothing less than misanthropy.

Mao: Only from misanthropy can come generosity. The man who does not despise the world does not know how much it is to be pitied and loved.

I: Loved?

Mao: Yes, the way one may love homeless cats —but there is a limit to this analogy. While cats demand nothing of you and give nothing in return, men will suck out your brains and guts and ask you to pull them off while doing it.

I: What is to be done?

Mao: Learn a pleasant tune to whistle.

Interpreter: Yes, the tune you now whistle is one you've rehearsed for ages. It may be pleasant to you, but frankly, I hate it.

Mao: Your pretended honesty and boldness is vulgar and bores me. If it weren't that you were more frightened of my wife than of me, you'd be whistling the same tune.

I: Have you seen Godard's *La Chinoise*?

Mao: Yes. But I have been terrifically unimpressed. I find the interviews dull and irrelevant, and Godard's fiction that the film is a work in progress does not excuse nor aesthetically conceal the irrelevancy. For Godard the interview has become a convention, an ossification of what once was

a fluid technique; *La Chinoise* has no tension, no internal struggle, no dialectic, and
hence, it is a bore. I do think Godard means
well, and I have enjoyed other films of his.

I: Which?

Mao: *Breathless, Vivre Sa Vie, Made in U. S. A.*
Breathless perfectly captures the bitchery
of modern bourgeois women thrill-seekers.
Women disaffected, unnatural, women
whose life charge is expressed in their
ovaries only. And the young man is the
perfect expression of the third-rate punk,
the natural offspring of a decadent society
and its myths. What a waste . . . Belmondo
might have been a perfect Red Guard
youth, a fine revolutionary . . . in short, the
best kind of human being. Instead, look at
what all that energy went into: cheap violence, for the possession of ephemeral
thrills and for the re-enacting of another's
personality. The archetype of this was in
itself a fiction, a rôle. Godard's *Breathless*
is one of the *best* statements in contemporary art, of the sickness of modern Western
capitalist society. Jean Seberg is the
American bitch-killer. Belmondo, poor
man, is the expression of the more romantic cast of mind searching for some vehicle
of personality in which to live. Seberg is
soul-less, bland, colorless, unloving, white;
she is America's twentieth-century Moby
Dick, the White Killer, malign and impersonal. She is America! I half love her. (Mao
laughed; his interpreter giggled.)

Godard in *Breathless* is good and fresh,
half in love with his characters. He likes
Belmondo and even her a bit; he is taken
by their youth and charm and free life, but

he is repulsed by them and what has created them: Godard here expressed the perfect tension of the revolutionary artist who lives in a transitional phase of bourgeois culture. You should read Kenneth Burke's essay on the drama of Odets in either *Philosophy of Literary Form*, I think, or in *Counterstatement*.

Godard's contradictions are wholesome and accurate with regard to his condition in bourgeois culture. But films like *Made in U.S.A.* or *La Chinoise* show him uncertain in his *instincts*. He is now the Oscar Wilde of cinema imagery.

I: Do you object to the satire on youth in the film *La Chinoise*?

Mao: Yes. For satire must never be directed against the class whose aspirations you share—only against the enemy.

I: Perhaps Godard wanted to adjust or to expose the incorrect thinking of the youth whose revolutionary ideals have no application in France at this time.

Mao: Youth is never reactionary; youth is progressive in time and hence always in the avant-garde, hence *never* wrong in spirit, hence *never* to be satirized, especially in a culture in which the reactionary forces are in power and have the guns.

I: I see.

Mao: Besides, "France at this time," to use your phrase, may be exactly the place for youth like those in *La Chinoise*. But that brings into prophecy, not aesthetics, although the two are so allied!

I: Prophecy and aesthetics?

Mao: Yes. Obviously.

I: Earlier you spoke of the American artists

Morris, Judd, et cetera. What do you find
in their work?

Mao: We see in these artists and in painters like
Reinhardt and Olitski and Kelly — though
here the linguistic paraphrase of their work
veers dangerously close to critical solip-
sism—an Oriental bent, a dialectic predi-
cated on the desire to say a great deal, the
ineffable, in fact, by saying next to nothing.

I: Ineffable?

Mao: Ineffable because the sentiments and ideas
the work emanates are at once inclusive of
all thoughts that can be linguistically expressed: all history, all the past, present,
and future; and they include all that cannot be linguistically expressed: the *meaning* known intuitively, transcendentally of
all that is inexplicable.

I: Do you care to say more?

Mao: Pragmatically speaking, I like the opulent
severity of this art, Minimal or ABC, because it both fills the imagination with the
baroque by way of dialectical reaction to
the absolute starkness of the object, and
denudes the false in art and in life. Their
work is like The Long March, a victory over
space and time, a triumph of the necessary
over the unnecessary, and, above all, it is
like Marxism, or should I say like He-
raclitus . . . .

I: Yes?

Mao: A Morris or Judd sculpture/thing, say, is
its own ever-formulating thesis, antithesis,
and synthesis; it takes into account nothing
of history (except by its location in present
history), destroys or is intolerant of senti-
mentality and stock response, and thus is
excellent for inspiring and promulgating

socialist morality. Keats's Grecian urn is theoretically what an archetypal Minimal sculpture is, but Keats's urn is a Morris sculpture only on the level of saying: Keats tells us, "Look, this urn is omnipresent in space and infinite in time." But no real Grecian urn is that, except when it is devoid of all iconography, all paraphrasable material. An archetypal Minimal object is more like Wallace Stevens's glass jar resting in a wilderness, an artifact of eternity.

I: I find your interest in this art astonishing. Both the work and your involvement in it seem a contradiction of everything you have said or written. Frankly, I'm amazed.

Mao: Excuse me. A qualification of what I have just said: Actually their work is not like The Long March, for that represents struggle as a linear event in time. No. Their work is closer to the Great Harmony, in which dialectical tension and contradictions are in perfect stasis and equilibrium. When society attains the social, political, and economic stage that a Minimal sculpture reaches aesthetically, then mankind will have achieved the Great Harmony.

I: How can you condone, even extol works of art that bear no relation to objective reality?

Mao: What doesn't bear relation to objective reality?

I: The kind of art we were discussing.

Mao: Indeed it does. It is its own reality, its own subject and object.

Interpreter: (Interrupting) Do you mean that a square or a box or a giant grey round portable swimming pool without a bottom *is* reality?

Mao: It is the objectification of itself, the materialization of its own transcendental reality.

Interpreter: (Hotly) This is too much mystification for me. To be honest, Chairman Mao, hearing all this talk from you confuses me and disturbs me. What about Socialist Realism, what about . . . .

Mao: I forgive you this interruption. I will say only that Socialist Realism, all that we are now doing, all our banners, our posters of Red workers with caps, all our murals of marching Red armies and peasants, our entire art now is myth-derived. Our Social Realists are cartoonists of myths. And perhaps one day you will shut up while your betters are talking.

I: Chairman Mao, perhaps I might ask your opinion on birth control.

Mao: Shut up. And you, Lin Tang, I trust you will run off to Mrs. Mao and . . . tattle on me for my incorrect thinking; I suppose you will now go and do that after lunch, you decayed chopstick.

Interpreter: Forgive me. I shall be still, Chairman Mao.

I: Have you seen Dali's Mao/Marilyn?

Mao: Photos only, naturally, but it did interest me.

I: One of the American critics called the work vulgar. Do you agree?

Mao: No. Dali understood the relation between sexual power or sexual magnetism, and sexual myth, for the myth of Mao is sexual, political, et cetera. Marilyn is the feminine Mao; she is, dialectically speaking, the victim, the exploited, that what-would-have-been Mao had he lived in the United States and been a beautiful woman. Mao/Marilyn would be an interesting person, I think.

I: What are your plans for the future?

Mao: I'm an old man who wants to dream the remaining days away. Yet I can't take a nice healthy crap without some fanatic bowing to the stool and singing: "Oh, our great Chairman Mao has again fertilized the world." What was all my hard work for, if I can't fill my last hours with serenity and nonproductive contemplation?

I: Yes. That would be something.

Mao: "For who is the true critic but he who bears within himself the dreams, and ideas, and feelings of myriad generations, and to whom no form of thought is alien, no emotional impulse obscure? And who the true man of culture, if not he who by fine scholarship and fastidious rejection has made instinct self-conscious and intelligent, and can separate the work that has distinction from the work that has it not, and so by contact and comparison makes himself master of the secrets of style and school, and understands their meanings, and listens to their voices, and develops that spirit of disinterested curiosity which is the real root, as it is the real flower, of the intellectual life, and thus attains to intellectual clarity; and, having learned 'the best that is known and thought in the world,' lives—it is not fanciful to say so—with those who are the immortals?

"Yes, ... the contemplative life, the life that has for its aim not *doing* but *being,* and not *being* merely, but *becoming* — that is what the critical spirit can give us. The gods live thus: either brooding over their own perfection, as Aristotle tells us, or as

Epicurus fancied, watching with the calm
eyes of the spectator the tragi-comedy of
the world that they have made. We, too,
might live like them, and set ourselves to
witness with appropriate emotions the var-
ied scenes that man and nature afford. We
might make ourselves spiritual by detach-
ing ourselves from action, and become perfect by the rejection of energy. It has often
seemed to me that Browning felt something
of this. Shakespeare hurls Hamlet into active life, and makes him realize his mission
by effort. Browning might have given us a
Hamlet who would have realized his mission by thought. Incident and event were to
him unreal or unmeaning. He made the soul
the protagonist of life's tragedy, and looked
on action as the one undramatic element
of a play. . . . From the high tower of thought
we can look out at the world. Calm, and
self-centered, and complete, the aesthetic
critic contemplates life, and no arrow
drawn at a venture can pierce between the
joints of his harness. He at least is safe. He
has discovered how to live.

"Is such a mode of life immoral? Yes, all
the arts are immoral, except those baser
forms of sensual or didactic art that seek
to excite to action of evil or of good. For
action of every kind belongs to the sphere
of ethics. The aim of art is simply to create
a mood. Is such a mode of life unpractical?
Ah! It is not so easy to be unpractical as the
ignorant Philistine imagines . . . . There is
no country in the world so much in need of
unpractical people as this country of ours.
With us, thought is degraded by its constant associations with practice. Who that

moves in the stress and turmoil of actual existence, noisy politician, or brawling social reformer, or poor, narrow-minded priest, blinded by the sufferings of that unimportant section of the community among whom he has cast his lot, can seriously claim to be able to form a disinterested intellectual judgment about any one thing? Each of the professions means a prejudice. The necessity for a career forces everyone to take sides. We live in the age of the overworked, and the under-educated; the age in which people are so industrious that they become absolutely stupid. And, harsh though it may sound, I cannot help saying that such people deserve their doom. The sure way of knowing nothing about life is to try to make oneself useful."

I: My dear Chairman, this meeting with you has made me older; all your thoughts have given me the desire to be inert, to live without thought or fear of the days ahead, as they age me one by one. You have lived your struggle, have made your long march. But what can quiet in old age mean to us who have been not on The Long March but on the short stroll?

Interpreter: You have done all right for yourself, Mao. It's always like that; old men who have lived fiercely always talk about dying in peace, but it is only talk. They're troublemakers to the end!

Mao: I wish the old days were here again, say 1902; then I'd have you beaten to your nerves with a ragged bamboo pole.

I: That's more likely, Chairman Mao. At least I shall go away with memory of your irascibility.

Mao: These outbursts are only to amuse you.

I: Then, you'd like me to believe in your dream of a pastoral old age?

Mao: "I have a strange longing for the great simple primaeval things, such as the sea, to me no less of a mother than the Earth. It seems to me that we all look at Nature too much, and live with her too little. I discern great sanity in the Greek attitude. They never chattered about sunsets, or discussed whether the shadows on the grass were really mauve or not. But they saw that the sea was for the swimmer, and the sand for the feet of the runner. They loved the trees for the shadow that they cast, and the forest for its silence at noon. The vineyard-dresser wreathed his hair with ivy that he might keep off the ray of the sun as he stooped over the young shoots, and for the artist and the athlete, the two types that Greece gave us, they plaited with garlands the leaves of the bitter laurel and of the wild parsley, which else had been of no service to men.

"We call ours a utilitarian age, and we do not know the uses of any single thing. We have forgotten that water can cleanse, and fire purify, and that the Earth is mother to us all. As a consequence our art is of the moon and plays with shadows, while Greek art is of the sun and deals directly with things. I feel sure that in elemental forces there is purification, and I want to go back to them and live in their presence."

Epigraph	Shakespeare, *Antony and Cleopatra*
p. 2	Jack London, *Iron Heel*
p. 3–5	Parody of Dos Passos/Steinbeck
p. 6–7	Jack London, *Iron Heel* (pp.241–42)
p. 7–14	Nathaniel Hawthorne, *The Marble Faun*, chapter: *"A Sculptor's Studio"*
p. 14–15	London, *Iron Heel* (pp. 243–45)
p. 16–17	John William De Forest, *Miss Ravenel's Conversion*
p. 17–18	*Iron Heel*
p. 21–22	*Miss Ravenel's Conversion* (p. 259)
p. 22–24	Mao Tse Tung, "Strategy in China's Revolutionary War" (sec V), Selected Works, Vol I, Peking
p. 25	Rendering of Faulkner—allusions to *Light in August, The Bear, Sanctuary*
p. 29	Herman Melville, "Roman Statuary"
p. 32–33	James Fenimore Cooper, *The Bravo* (section in which boatmen come to the canal), Chapter 22 of the one-volume edition, or Chapter 7, Vol II of the two-volume edition: opening lines of the chapter
p. 33	Cooper, *The Bravo*, Chapter 24 of one-volume edition; or Chapter 9, Vol II of two-volume edition

Postscript 2005

A Brief (Autobiographical) History of
The Adventures of Mao on the Long March

1950s. I was nineteen when I met Albert Halper, author of the long forgotten, proletarian novel, *Union Square*. I had only met maybe one or two published authors, my teachers at college who did not count in my idea of being a writer, mostly because they wore jackets and ties and were not outlaws, as I had expected and wanted and in some retrograde way still want artists to be. Halper was a burly guy, with a big meaty handshake, and he looked tough my idea of a merchant seaman or a union organizer. A hero, that is.

I hear you're writing a novel, kid, he said.

I was, I said. In fact, I was. A novel about Mexico and love and sex and death (what else?) and drinking tequila and seeing bullfights and being, as I was and always am, alone.

Good for you, he said. It's your first book, no one's looking over your shoulder, so throw everything in it, even the kitchen sink. It took a long time for that idea to sink in, so to speak.

1969. Albert Halper's suggestion finally takes, but it isn't the kitchen sink I throw into my novel-in-progress but a library of my readings. Which, at that moment, was mainly in early Nineteenth century American Literature, as I was writing along with the Mao novel my Ph.D. thesis on James Fenimore Cooper.

Mark Twain, in two essays separated by twenty years, had a wonderful time destroying Cooper, mocking his on again, off again verisimilitude, Cooper opting to use a distant cousin rather than the exact word needed for the occasion. For all of Twain's derision, Cooper was a good writer for what he wanted to do. He kept his characters apace with the narrative, as it sped along, darkening as it went. You had little time to notice how wooden his characters were as they flashed by, fleeing from their pursuers in the dark forest.

Cooper was even a fine writer when he had the chance, as when he made his revisions to *The Bravo*, his political novel set in eighteenth century Venice, a republic in name only, as it devolved into an oligarchy, which was his fear for America. He subtitled his book, *A Cautionary Tale*. An obvious tag, but he was anxious that his readers get the point. I realized only much later how much Cooper affected me in the writing of *The Long March*. His cautionary note, his injured sense of the darkness and the lies beneath the bright public façade of noble declarations runs through my book.

1970. *Mao* is finished and sent about to various and many publishers. Rejected by many and various publishers. The consensus: Publisher regrets; It's not a novel. Opening me to the question: What is a novel? A question never answered, a conversation never held.

Same unanswered question in 2002, when, on a committee for a prestigious literary prize, I propose for consideration a novel by a veteran avant-garde writer, in which every sentence of its four hundred or so pages is interrogatory. It's not a novel, and we can't consider it, the committee chair said. Unless you want to make a special category for originality. More on this later.

Susan Sontag reads my manuscript and, without my solicitation, asks her publisher to reconsider *Mao*. It had been turned down by an editor at her house who, weeks earlier at lunch, informed me that my novel was a cold, Andy Warhol put-on. Heartless, I think he added.

Decide to self-publish the novel. Have it printed in Gibraltar or someplace on the cheap. Thinking it's better to have copies to send to friends than keep the manuscript in a drawer where, unlike principle in a bank, a book grows old without interest.

I ask my friend Roy Lichtenstein to do the book jacket. We are old friends. I loved his work from the early Sixties and we shared similar views about art. He once said to me that most artists have a preconception about what a work of art should look like before they put a mark on the canvas. Thus they make the same painting better or worse than others over and again. Ditto, I said, for most fiction writing. Thus the endless repetitions of well-made stories in well-pressed sentences. Stories that usually begin with the protagonist's meditation on his or her manicured lawn in the suburbs and end with an insight into the nature of his or her white ennui.

Roy agrees to help me get *The Long March* published understanding very well that innovation is more readily accepted in the visual than in the literary world. Nothing has changed in that department.

October. I'm saved from the route of self-publication. Citadel Press will publish my novel on the condition that Roy make a lithograph of Mao for a deluxe edition. It's a simple deal and Roy understands it: His edition will make the trade publication possible. Without my dear friend's generosity, *The Adventures of Mao on the Long March* would never have been published.

Roy creates, with the designers John Garrigan and Susanna Torre, a special Plexiglas box edition with a lithograph (23 1/16 x 16 inches) of Mao's head. 150 signed copies. The specially designed book with its accordion-like, wrap-around pages signed by me.

Roy received not a penny in advance for his work and at the end, not a mill of profit. And, as it turned out, his pioneer image of the dangerous Mao was usurped by another artist, when the Great Helmsman was later tamed into a celebrity icon, like Che.

1971. Who will come after us first, Roy asked me when the book was finally published, the Left or the Right?

I ask Roy's art dealer, Leo Castelli, to show the special edition with the Mao litho. He declines. Mao is our enemy, he says. He was right there, of course, but perhaps not for the same reasons I would have then thought.

I run into Andy Warhol, who asks if I would like to trade the Lichtenstein *Mao* for something of his. I say sure. But then, in my fashion, procrastinate, keeping in mind all the while my intention to make the trade. Then one day, years later, Andy dies and the trade is off.

1971–1972. There is a very good review by Thomas Lask, a conservative literary critic, in the daily *New York Times*. Other good reviews and some attention follows. And some generous words from other writers.

John Updike favorably reviews *Mao on the*
Long March in *The New Yorker*. Editor who called
my novel a Warhol put-on phones me to have
lunch. Says he made a mistake. Maybe you didn't
I say, maybe the critics did. First and only time
in my life I made so quick a riposte. An editor's
retraction being the dream of every rejected
writer. Read Jack London's *Martin Eden* for such
a dream come true. Read it anyway. And while
you're at it, read his futuristic *The Iron Heel*,
parts of which I embedded in *Mao*, for the flavor
of class warfare between the people and the
oligarchs.

1972. Diana Vreeland, the legendary *Vogue* Magazine editor, cables me in Paris to congratulate me
for my scoop interview with Mao. She would like
me to do another for *Vogue*. Painful to tell her that
the interview was imagined. I propose she send
me to China anyway. Maybe a fashion shoot with
Mao among a bevy of models holding the *Little
Red Book*.

Citadel Press cannot market and cannot sell
most of the special box edition. The Plexiglas box
is broken; the remaining prints returned to Roy,
the books to me. Maybe 15 or 20 copies of the
special edition still survive intact.

February. I see on TV President Nixon step off
the plane in The People's Republic of China and
shake Premier Cho En Lai's hand. Nixon is soon
on his way to meet Chairman Mao. I turn to my
cat, Nicolino, and say, that's the end of the Chinese Revolution. Having suspected it had ended
long before. Nicolino, as usual, in matters of politics and love, remains sagely silent. I promise to
include him as a character in all my future novels.
Promise so far kept.

November. Andy Warhol shows his Mao silk screen series at the Leo Castelli Gallery. To great acclaim. No one better than Andy to feel the zeitgeist. Good for him. In any case, he and Roy had made their own quiet revolutions, making us restructure our ideas of what is the subject matter for art, and thus revitalizing our idea of both art and life.

1973. Receive a scrawly, handwritten letter from Raymond Queneau, the novelist, poet, mathematician, and editor at Gallimard. A writer I adore for his wit and ironic wisdom, for making, along with Celine, art from the lingo of the street. Queneau asks to publish *Mao on the Long March*. I'm sure this is a hoax perpetrated by one of my Parisian friends. Very funny, I say to her on the phone. I may have added more words but transatlantic calls were costly then.

1975. *Les Adventures de Mao Pendant la Longue Marche*, published by Gallimard. Translated by Maurice Rambaud. Now I understand how Poe can read better in French than in English.

1977. *Las adventuras de Mao en la larga marcha* published by Ediciones Fundamentos. The publisher is a young writer, from Madrid, Julian Rios. Now he's an older writer of original and beautiful novels. When I go to live in Paris, he cautions me about all the Proustitutes I may meet there and how that might affect my prose style.

Marion Boyars reprints *Mao* in England and America. Marion is a small, passionate woman who keeps all her authors in print: more valuable to a writer than gold. When she died a few years ago, the new publisher offers to sell me the remaining books, otherwise, for considerations of

storage, they must be shredded. After the lack of
success of *Walden*, Thoreau said he had a library
of some two thousand books, all of them his.
Writers must have had much more room to store
their returned books in those days.

1950s: A backward glance: A young man drops
out of high school with the idea of becoming an
artist. What medieval romances did to make Don
Quixote leave home and rush windmills, *Lust for
Life* and *Moon and Sixpence* did to make this boy
dream of living in Paris, in a garret, above a cafe,
etc. But for the moment he is living in the Bronx,
with his mother, and working odd jobs. He also
writes obscure poetry. Which from time to time
he sends far away to Manhattan, to New Directions, the Parnassus for all avant-garde dream-
ers. Maybe he's the American Rimbaud? He's
young enough to be. In any case, in aesthetic
matters, he'd rather, he says, roam the mountains
with the outlaws than march in step with the
army. He waits and waits and eventually a note
arrives, all the way from that magical island that
could also be Paris, thanking him for sending the
poems which are rejected and please consider
sending them more poems in the future.

2005. New Directions Classics republishes *The
Adventures of Mao on the Long March*.
    I look back and wonder where these thirty-four
years have disappeared since Mao was first published. And more, I wonder if that young man kept
faith with his idea of living in the mountains
with the outlaws. With not surrendering his be-
lief that the novel is a flexible, elastic and ever
re-inventible form. That fiction is the supreme
poetry, when it sheds itself of prose.
    Let a hundred flowers grow, Mao once said,

134   seeming to invite a multitude of voices to contend in the new, revolutionary society. But he really meant to hear only one voice, to see only one flower flourish, his own.

All other flowers did not fare so well in his soil. In our world, flowers of various complexity and beauty grow in uncensored riot, some rising higher than others to the sun. Some may find it expeditious to plant those sun-climbing flowers, which rise so quickly and are thus easily seen and enjoyed by so many, myself as well. But I still find myself searching for those mysterious, rare flowers born afield, in the mountains, where outlaws are yet said to live.